LUCY
in the
SKYE

Carolina Giacobone

authorHOUSE®

AuthorHouse™ UK
1663 Liberty Drive
Bloomington, IN 47403 USA
www.authorhouse.co.uk
Phone: 0800.197.4150

Published by AuthorHouse 12/08/2016

ISBN: 978-1-5246-6381-0 (sc)
ISBN: 978-1-5246-6382-7 (hc)
ISBN: 978-1-5246-6380-3 (e)

Dedication

To those with voices as their friends.
To those with blackness in their heart.
To those whose who've lost their joy and faith.
May this story bring you light.

Carolina

CHAPTER ONE

A DAY IN MY LIFE

May 2005

I woke up to the familiar tickling sensation down my hands. I opened one eye and saw the pool of crimson, as I'd expected. I lazily closed it again, drained of all life, until the surrounding red was replaced by black.

* * *

This time, the familiar sound of the drop of the intravenous line awoke me. It is very hard to get your bearings when you have been doped up for several hours. At least I assumed I had been in hospital for a considerable time, but my memory was still a cloud of haze and tablets. My eyes complained at the brightness of the pristine hospital room. Okay, everything was clean and smelled good, so I wasn't in a Psych institution. Not yet at least.

"Lucy, you are awake!" Newsflash. "How are you feeling?"

My aunt burst into tears as she squeezed my ribs. I was a petite 1.58m ginger 20-year-old, give me some room woman. "Peachy, Maria. Just peachy." I sighed. "Where's mom?"

"She's getting coffee. She stayed up all night holding your hand Lucy." More like holding my bandaged wrists. "We were worried sick!" My aunt gave me another quick hug and wiped her tears. I patted her back.

"There, there". My aunt was cool, I really liked her. She was sweet, and supportive, and always tried to be understanding when I went *coo coo*. Unlike mom. Not that I blamed her. Or maybe I did. I definitely did.

The first time I hallucinated I was 13. It wasn't a fully formed voice; it was more like a whisper. I was sure it was my grandmother speaking to me from Heaven; 13 years old, grieving her loss, naive enough to believe in God and such. My mom and the school psychologist assured me it was a normal part of grief, hearing your loved ones, but their furtive glances and the biweekly appointments with the therapist said otherwise. That voice never came back. But others followed.

I wasn't worried at all by the strange workings of my mind. I knew I was different, but not cliché different. Special different. My mom was evidently upset by me not turning into an ideal, valedictorian teenager. She tried very poorly to hide her concern for my bizarreness, which always gave me a guilty sense of pleasure.

I can't say I didn't enjoy torturing my mom a little. My psychoanalyst, way more bonkers than I was, was completely convinced I was punishing my poor mother for the disappearance of my father. But I never heard my father's voice, I barely remembered it anyway. My psychoanalyst used to say abandonment is even harder to process than death, and that might have been the only wise thing that came out of her preposterously red lips.

At 15, my lovely friend Asia introduced me to the bliss of booze. She had sneaked into her father's office and snatched what we later found out was a very fine bottle of Talisker whisky. I was a curious child, what can I say, it was more of a science experiment for me. Maybe a bottle of whisky would silence the voices.

The alcohol numbed my senses and gave me a sense of relief. But then came the concern, what if all that free sugar turned into fat and piled up around my tiny waist? Clearly the easiest solution would be to cut down on the food, come on, it's not like food was essential

Wednesday morning: yoga and meditation. If they made us wear robes and leggings, I would make them swallow the mats.

Thursday morning: family day. Ding ding ding! We've found the winner for worst nightmare!

Friday morning: group therapy. Okay, rephrasing that last statement. Friday might have been a Freddy Krueger kind of nightmare.

And then individual therapy every afternoon, with Psychiatrist, Psychologist, Occupational Therapist and Social Worker, in that blessed order. And the icing on the cake…a movie session on Friday afternoon! Why didn't I just *die*?

I turned to my mother and mumbled through gritted teeth. "If you get me out of here now, I promise I'll clean the house without setting it on fire." She slapped my arm and gave me a tiny push.

"She's ready," my mom said to the director. "Behave, you little rascal," she half-joked. "Please, do it for me." She gave me a peck on the cheek and tried to hide her tears as she exited Hell's lobby.

"Good, follow me Lucy. Is it okay if I call you that?" I hate you.

"Yes, Doctor Whelan." Is it okay if I call you Lucifer?

She showed me the common dining room, the "movie" room (1998 called, they want their TV and VCR back), and the rooms for art therapy and group therapy. Yoga and the physical activities were held in a large park outside the building, with a small pond shaded by the canopy of a Weeping willow.

"Breakfast is at 8.30 am, lunch at 12.30 and then a snack at 4pm. Do you have any questions so far?" I was wondering if people preferred to drown in the pond or to hang themselves from the tree, but I figured Doctor Whelan wouldn't take too amicably to my curiosity. I shook my head.

"I will show you our offices now and then lead you to your room so you can unpack. You'll be pleased to know that since we are a Day care facility, you won't have a roommate for the week you are staying overnight." Delighted. I stuck to nodding. "The patients are having breakfast at the moment, but you'll be able to join them at 10am for the Pilates session in the garden. I'll see you at 2pm for our first meeting."

I tried to speak, but no sound came out. Maybe she had put a spell on me. I cleared my throat. "What am I supposed to do in my spare time?"

She gave me that huge smile that I already hated so much. "Anything you want, of course, within the rules. We have quite a vast collection of movies, books and board games, and you can always try to socialize with the other patients."

I don't know what tempted me more, if playing chess with one of the Schizophrenic's voices or *Cluedo* with a real psycho killer. The safest option would definitely be to watch *Rainman* or *Forrest Gump* with the retards.

I unpacked as slowly as I could. The room was medium-sized and quite lively, thankfully the bed beside mine was empty. Although I regretted I wouldn't have a partner-in-crime. Maybe she could have been a cool Bipolar chick who would help me nick a box antipsychotics and escape this pothole.

At 9.55, a nurse came looking for me. She wasn't grinning as forcefully as the director or the receptionist, quite understandably. Who in their right mind would want to rally around schizos, psychos, bipolars, addicts, and autists like damned cattle? Her name was Dana. She led me to back yard without uttering a single word. I definitely liked her.

OH MY GOD. At first glance, I spotted at least two dozens of people lying on the grass with their legs and arms outstretched. It was a sight I would never forget, especially because half of them were doing it completely wrong, and the other half was just muttering to themselves. Welcome to aerobics for the crazy.

"Okay people, listen up!" the instructor yelled. Don't get your hopes up buddy, they were probably more interested in the chit-chatter going on in their own heads. "Cleveland blessed us with this lovely day in the middle of May, so today we'll do a little cardio." Good, maybe I'd die of a heart attack.

"I have to say, this was quite a lot of fun in a twisted kind of way", a guy said to my ear when the session was over. Sweat was trickling down my freckled forehead. My ginger curls were pasted to the sides of my face like I had never moved a limb in my entire life before. Well, probably I hadn't.

"Oh yeah, nothing beats jogging with a bunch of wackos," I responded, still gasping for air.

He laughed softly. "Well, you can't be too…right up there yourself if you are stuck here with us." He pointed at his head.

I raised an eyebrow. "You'd be surprised." He wasn't exactly good looking, but he was tall, very tall. Later on in life, as I would try to remember his face when I missed it, he would look like the most beautiful man on Earth.

"I'm Will Cadillac." He outstretched his hand. "Recovering addict."

"Lucy Skye, Borderline Personality Disorder with a tinge of micro psychotic episodes and a pinch of suicide attempts," I shook his hand. He didn't seem surprised by my response.

"Lucy Sky? As Lucy in the Sky with Diamonds?"

I gave him the finger as we gathered our mats and proceeded to the common room. "Ha-ha, Will Cadillac. You are full of cheesy clichés, aren't you? A 20 something year old admitted for drinking too much so that he could rebel against his parents and appear to be cool with his loser buddies?"

We slouched in a double couch, where a nurse handed us two cups of iced tea. The rest of the crazies had already taken what I assumed were their usual positions around the room.

"Wow, you suck at reading people," he snickered. "More like a 22-year-old who started liking codeine, clonazepam and muscle relaxants a little too much to deal with his crippling social anxiety and the sudden death of his parents in a car crash."

"You are pathetic if you think that will make me feel sorry for you," I scoffed. "And who gets addicted to muscle relaxants anyway?"

"Hey, at least I never used anything IV! Kudos for me!"

I wouldn't give him the pleasure of laughing at his joke, not yet anyway. It was way too soon to give into his quirky charms. "I'm glad I won't get hepatitis from you then." He blushed a little. So much for dealing with his social anxiety. "Lucy is short for Lucila, by the way."

"That's interesting," he said. He genuinely seemed interested, oh my. Poor guy. "Are your parents Latino?"

This time I laughed, hard. "My mom was born in Argentina, but her family moved here to the US when she was 6. And my dad is Irish."

"Is that why you have a hint of an Irish accent? It's quite weird to hear it in Cleveland, to tell you the truth."

I shrugged my shoulders. "I guess it's the only thing he left me."

Will looked out the window, sipping his iced tea. I followed suit. I appreciated silence, sometimes. The rest of the time it just reminded me I was an empty bottle, stranded in a sea of waves, with no message hidden in its core.

CHAPTER TWO

THE BOTTLE, THE FLOWER AND THE UNICORN

*M*y drawing looked more like a pony than a unicorn, but hey, the art therapist said we could draw whatever identified us. So there you go.

"Is that supposed to be a unicorn?" Will laughed.

"I'm getting tired of you. You are boring. Go bother someone else."

He laughed again. Apparently, he was immune to my borderline insults. "The horn gave it away."

I took a peek at his drawing and almost died. "Is that a gigantic penis?" I yelled, purposely. It was obviously a building of some sort, but never mind. I was helping him deal with his social anxiety. Kind of.

"Bitch," he whispered, crimson all over. "It's the Agbar Tower in Barcelona. I was an architect student before I came here."

"Thanks for that vital piece of information." I gave him the thumbs up. "How come you feel identified by a penis-shaped building? Are you attending your therapy sessions?"

"Probably more than you are, I bet you just doze off in the middle of the conversation." He guessed correctly. Damn it, I didn't like being predictable.

"You're wrong," I lied. "The psychologist says I'm making progress." A massive, blunt lie.

"Considering your first week you drew a glass bottle, last week a dead flower and this week you moved on to animals, mythical or not, I'd say your psychologist is right." It was a little sweet that he remembered my drawings. "Who is your therapist?"

"Mr. Hawkins."

"Oh, and Dr. Whelan is your Psychiatrist." He whistled. "Wow, you scored the elite team!"

"Yay! Do I get a medal for crazy of the week?" Will laughed, that soft chuckle that managed to fill my dark void for a few seconds. "So why Barcelona? Have you been?"

"Nah," Will said, with an obvious air of disappointment. "The farthest I've been is Mexico. You?"

"No, not to Barcelona. But I used to go to Galway in Ireland every summer for a month or two to see my dad. Well, as long as my mom let me really." I gulped and stared fixedly at the unicorn. Not that this was a difficult topic for me. It was super mega digested, evidently. "We loved going to Salthill Beach, he'd chase me around with an ice-cream cone until I was out of breath." Will smiled, the truest smile I had seen in days. "But then my dad bailed when I was 11, he sent me a lovely card full of good wishes."

"What happened?"

"I have no idea," I responded truthfully. "At least I get to go every year to Argentina for the winter holidays now. We don't really have any close family there, they are all here in Cleveland, but I guess it's my mom's way to make it up to me. And we get to practice our Spanish."

"She sounds cool," Will said nonchalantly.

"She's an accountant, Will." I smirked. "But well, going to Argentina beats building snowmen in Tremont Park for Christmas."

Will looked taken aback. "Wait, you live in Tremont?" I nodded, confused by his sudden enthusiasm. "I think I know you!"

The art therapist clapped. "Okay people," *crazy* people darling, I thought to myself, "time to share your drawings."

*   *   *

Will's words stayed with me, but I didn't see him again until Friday's group therapy.

"Lucy!" the group therapist called out. Maybe there was another Lucy in the group. Please let it be another Lucy. "You've been awfully quiet for the past two weeks. Why don't you share something with us today?"

Everyone in the circle turned their heads to fix their eyes on me. Maybe this was one of the Circles of Hell Dante had described.

"Share?" I echoed, as if I didn't understand English. Maybe if I pretended to be mentally challenged, the therapist would leave me alone. She hardly ever made the retards speak.

"Yes, how about…your dreams?"

"Oh, sorry, I don't dream much," I confessed, shrugging. "The mortal combo of antipsychotic, anxiolytic and mood stabilizer pretty much knocks me out." I heard Will's soft laugh.

The group therapist was growing impatient with me. I didn't even remember her name. "I meant something intimate, like your dreams, aspirations, goals in life."

"Oh, I get you sister." Now Will chuckled openly. "Well, you see, I've always dreamt of having superpowers." The therapist raised her eyebrows, but signaled me to continue. "Okay, so you know the Halliwell witches, right?" Dead silence. "Prue, Piper, Phoebe and Paige? Anyone?" No *Charmed* fans amongst the wackos, what? I definitely didn't expect that. "Never mind. Prue had telekinesis and astral projection, Piper freezes time and blows things up, Phoebe has visions of the future and the past, and Paige can teleport and heal. I want all of those powers." The therapist meant to interrupt me, but I was on a roll. "Phoebe could levitate and was an empath too, but she lost those powers in a witch trial. She was given the chance to earn them back, but the show is about to end, and she hasn't gotten them back yet. Talk about injustice!" I was gesturing madly, I bet the therapist was loving this.

"Okay Lucy, that's quite a lot of information to process, thank you for sharing. Would anyone else like to pick up on the topic raised… not superpowers, injustice I mean?"

Will raised his thumbs at me and I stuck my tongue back at him. Childish, cheesy, boring, sad excuse for a guy. Thank god I only had to endure two more hours of a pathetic movie in the afternoon, and then I would be free to go sulk in my misery in the confines of my home, while I concocted a plan to escape that hellish rut.

*   *   *

In the End by Linkin Park was blasting through my Ipod Shuffle when I felt the tap on my shoulder. You had to be shitting me!

"Damn you, Cadillac! Are you fucking following me? I knew you were a creep!"

Will slapped his forehead. "We are neighbors, you crazy ass… witch. I was sure I knew you from somewhere. Did you happen to have purple hair a few years ago?"

I sat back on the Tremont park bench. *My* bench. "I went through a phase, and violet is my favorite color, what can I say."

"Are you sure you moved on from that phase?" I threw him a murderous look. "Okay okay, my apologies, *sister.*"

"What the hell are you doing here anyway?" I turned off the Ipod.

"We live in the same apartment block. I come to the park when the weather's nice too. You don't own it, you know." I grabbed my face, faking surprise. "You are incurable, Skye."

A bright idea sparked in my brilliant head. Very red and always burning, just like Mars. I made room for him to sit next to me. I was sharing my sacred place. This had better pay off. "I need your help, bro."

"Only if you tell me what all those tattoos are about," he blurted out. I doubted he had planned on saying that, but maybe my impulsiveness was rubbing off on him. I was grand.

I hadn't shared this with anyone, ever. But for some reason, it didn't feel like an overexposed, intimate moment of revelation. I lowered the sleeves of my jersey.

"So my friend," although that was a bit of a stretch, "I have a bucket list."

"Tattooed on your body?" I nodded. This had certainly spiked his attention.

"The order is as follows, bear with me."

1. **Find my dad**: I showed him the tattoo of the shamrock in my right wrist.
2. **Try a hallucinogenic**: tattoo of a starry sky on my left shoulder.
3. **Fall in love at first sight**: tattoo of a heart with spikes just above my chest. He snickered at that one.
4. **See a unicorn**: tattoo of a purple unicorn on my right shoulder.
5. **Travel around the world**: tattoo of a tiny replica of the Earth on left ankle, with a flaming Argentine flag.
6. **Have a magical power**: tattoo of a Hindu eye at the back of my neck. I had to collect and pull up a huge amount of red curls to show him that one.
7. **Go to a nudist beach**: tattoo of a massive wave colliding with my collarbone.
8. **Do bungee jumping**: tattoo of a convoluted noose on the inside of my left arm. Beautifully adorned by the scars from the repeated self-cutting and burning with cigarette butts.
9. **Find peace**: tattoo of an olive tree on my waist.
10. **Save a life:** no tattoo for that one yet. Couldn't figure out what would represent that wish properly.

"Wow Skye, you never cease to impress me." He looked sincerely awestruck, and was scarlet all over.

"So... now that the truth is out in the open…" I held one of his hands and cradled it with both of mine. Either his were huge or mine were tiny. Or both. I stared into his hazel eyes. They were kind of cute, warm and sincere all over, just like he was. "Will, will you find the will to help me?"

He pretended to give it an insightful thought. "How could I resist a pretty girl who, on top of all her awesomeness, makes puns with my name?" I smiled, a true, honest smile. A sense of relief invaded me, making the tip of my fingers tingle. I hadn't experienced anything like it in a really long time...perhaps this is what something similar to joy felt like. "What do you need from me?"

"I NEED TO ESCAPE THAT WRETCHED LAME EXCUSE FOR A TREATMENT CENTER WILLIAM! ASAP, do you copy? ASAP!" I was tugging so hard on my hair, that tiny red curls were now decorating the park's immaculate grass.

"Whoa, back down there, Rambo," he said, sitting me back down. "I've been there for four months, and you've just started. You've only tried it for three weeks Skye."

"You think I don't know that?!?" I was standing up again. "I don't think you appreciate the graveness of my situation. IT FELT LIKE THREE DECADES, I see my life slipping through my fingers every time Mr. Hawkins makes me talk about my cutting and my body image issues!"

Will giggled. "You have body image issues? You're seriously messed up." I gave him a hard elbow on his ribs, but he barely budged. "You are a drama queen; did you know that?"

"Yes, a drama queen who needs money and tons of medication if she's going to go through with her plan."

He raised his hands. "Alright, you got me. Fill me in, crazy."

*   *   *

"Skye, I honestly don't think 800 hundred dollars will get you very far." Will was bouncing up and down on my double bed.

"They are my savings from my communion and my bloody confirmation. My mom's Catholic." I spat. "I also have the extension to my mom's credit and debit cards, that should help."

"You are still a little short on cash, still." He was now playing with one of those stupid stress balls.

"Could you PLEASE stop bouncing like that! And stay quiet, you're getting on my nerves."

"Like that's a challenge…" he muttered. "Okay, fine Lucy. I might, and the key word here being *might*, be able to procure you 2000 more."

My heart skipped a bit. "Are you serious??? Oh my god, I could almost hug you right now!"

"Please don't." He blocked my freckly outstretched arms. "I should be able to nick some money from the safe, and I have some savings from my summer jobs. I was meaning to save some more for my student loans, but my aunt and uncle are pretty well-off, and my parents left a considerable inheritance, so no worries there." He knew I would protest, so he kept on talking before I could intervene. "How are you on the passport area?"

"Ugh, got that one overly covered." I fetched a small bag in my bottom drawer and spilled out the contents on my bed. "I am officially an American, an Argentinean, and an Irish citizen. I highly doubt that's even legal."

"How did that happen?" Will asked, as he inspected my triple-threat passports.

"You see, my dad is Irish, and so are his parents. I was born in the US, but I lived since I was a baby in Galway, until my folks separated when I was 7 or 8. Then we came back to Cleveland. My mom is Argentine, but she moved to the US as a little girl when the 1976 dictatorship hit Argentina. So lovely me having been born here, and with that intricate family tree, allowed me to have American, Argentine and Irish passports."

"Hmmm…and which place do you consider home?" he asked, still browsing my numerous stamps. I had been asked so many stupid, useless questions in my life by all kinds of so-called professionals, but never that one.

I looked up and gazed at his hazel eyes. I shrugged and stared at the three passports. "Nowhere."

A knocking on my bedroom door awoke me from my stupor.

"Oh, Lucy! Is that your mom? What if she figures out what you're planning? Should I leave? Will she freak out if she sees a guy in your room?" Will was whispering frantically, pearls of sweat already shining in his pale forehead.

"You are insufferable, Cadillac," I complained. "I am pretty sure my mom will be delighted to see a decent-looking guy in my room for a change."

The knocking resumed. I opened the door to find, obviously, my mom standing there in her elegant suit and flawless hair. I could almost hear Will's jaw dropping to the floor. Yeah, yeah, my mom was drop dead gorgeous. She was called Olivia Cruz.

"Sweetie, hi, I'm done for the day," she announced cheerfully. My mom usually worked with her private accounting clients on Saturdays. She studied the scattered mess of maps, passports and travel guides over my bed. "What have you been up to?" She had that suspicious look I hated so much, it's not like I had stolen her razor again to scrape the skin off my thighs or something.

"Hi mom, this is Will Cadillac." I gave Will a push forward. He had dark circles of sweat in his armpits. Ewww Will, keep your anxiety in your pants. "We are working together in an assignment for our Art Therapy session. We are supposed to create a collage of our favorite places around the world." She was still wearing that stupid mask of suspicion. She had developed strong immunity to my lies by now. "You know, free your mind, envision the world, explore your soul, that kind of crap." Will gave her a scarlet nod.

"Fine," she finally agreed. "Are you staying over for dinner Will?"

He can't talk mom, he has crippling social anxiety and no clonazepam around. And you are a complete knocker.

"No, no, we are almost done." I smiled at my mom, before shouting at her that I demanded *milanesas a caballo* for dinner.

"Spoiled brat," I heard her mumble as she closed the door behind her perfectly round bum.

*   *   *

"I don't think this is a good idea Skye," Will whispered in a trembling voice. "Are you sure the nurses are on their break? Because I'm certainly not sure!"

It was Monday 10.15 am and pouring outside. That meant that physical activities were to be held in the indoor pool. I said I was on my period, so they allowed me to skip aqua gym for the crazies, and Will told the nurse he had a nasty cold. With those rosy cheeks and that gleaming face, I would have believed him too. Except he was sick in the head, not in the nose.

Most of the nurses would be having breakfast or overseeing the pool activities, so that no one attempted a coup and provoked a mass drowning suicide. It was the perfect time to execute part one of my plan. I hadn't devised part two yet, but I was very keen on improvising.

"Here Cadillac, take a clonazepam," I said, handing him a white, round tablet. We had snuck into the second floor's nurse's station, which was usually unsupervised because no one really ventured into the second floor. It had a small medication cabinet, but there was no way we could have broken into the pharmacy or any other of the nurse's isles.

"I can't, smartass. I'm on paroxetine and pregabaline, no benzodiazepines for me, remember?"

"Potatos, potatoes," I sneered. "Come on, hurry up, you find the quetiapine and I'll get the lamotrigine."

We had agreed with Dr. Whelan that there was no chance in Hell I would take the valproic acid again. It made me gain weight in uncomfortable places, like my cheeks (the four of them), and gave me teenager's acne. Dreadful. Not to mention the weekly blood tests. And I was adamant on the quetiapine, I had heard the olanzapine made you even fatter than the valproic acid. And then there was the haloperidol, it made me drool all over like that Lord of the Rings troll. So in the end, it was lamotrigine + quetiapine + lorazepam twice a day. I was lovely, ginger walking corpse.

"Done." Will showed me 6 blisters of quetiapine 100mg. "You take 50mg a day, right? And the blisters have 10 tablets each, so you should be good for 4 months or so."

"Glad the pregabaline doesn't affect your math," I joked. "I got the same for lamotrigine. Now on to the lorazepam."

Damn it. Footsteps were approaching. We both ducked and held our breath. I could almost feel Will's heart hammering out of his chest. Mine was pounding equally. "Is anybody there?" one of the nurses shouted. She tried the door, which we had wisely locked from the inside.

"Erm…I'm just preparing the medication for the 11 o'clock round, Daisy," Will said in a strangely grave voice. Was he putting on a black accent? My, my. He was full of surprises.

"Alright Kevin, but hurry up, aqua gym is almost over." We heard Daisy walk away from the station.

"Nicely done, bro," I joked, nudging him on the ribs. "Now find me some lorazepam and you'll be crowned savior of the day."

There was nothing magically heroic about Will, except for his ability to remain kind, compassionate, selfless, generous and understanding, even under the worst of circumstances.

CHAPTER THREE

MY BUCKET'S LIST NUMBER ONE

I never really had to say goodbye to anyone before. My dad did that part for me, my grandfather had died a year before I was born, and my grandmother died in hospital after a massive stroke when I was 13. I never knew my Irish grandparents, I had never changed schools, and all my family lived close by, to my misfortune.

People with curly hair want it straight. Short people dream of being tall, only children cry for baby brothers. I mostly liked my red, curly hair, my 1.58m, my extremely slender, freckled, and scarred physique, my big emerald eyes framed by ginger lashes. I particularly relished on not having any siblings. But I would have given anything, and I mean anything, to have been born in a different family.

My oldest uncle, Bruno, disgusted me with his pretentious suits and business lawyer talk. Nobody took you seriously Bruno, especially with that surgically enhanced wife of yours, Greta, and those very special twins you procreated together, Philip and Penelope. Philip was great, he had ADHD, so we connected on some level. But the girl, Penelope, she was the devil incarnate. At 9 years-old, she was already the queen of whatever lame parties they had at school, president of her class, and was nicknamed "Penelope Glamour." No wonder my uncle was an alcoholic. My mom was the middle sister, she has already been introduced and deserved less than two lines. My youngest aunt, Maria, was the acceptable one. With 31 years-old and an eating disorder on her back, she was the one closest to my age, and to my craziness for that matter. She had no children, because I highly suspected she was a lesbian, which left me with those twin scoundrels as my only cousins.

I pondered all of my family's mishaps as I traveled on the Amtrak train from Cleveland to New York. That wasn't my final destination, of course, but after some quick research, I had found that the easiest and cheapest way to fly to Europe was from JFK airport. There wasn't much to behold on the scenery passing me by, so I decided to open the box Will had given me before parting ways at the Day hospital. I had whispered in his ear *"I hope one day you let me ride your Cadillac"*, then hopped on a cab to the train station. I hadn't even looked back to see what I imagined was a scarlet face and a pair of nostalgic hazel eyes.

"Lucy in the Skye, I hope these presents bring you some comfort during your path to enlightenment. Sincerely, Will Cadillac. P.S: that sounded very much like Galadriel. My bad. Sunday 20ᵗʰ June, 2005."

I laughed out loud at his stupidity. The lady beside me threw me a menacing look. Fuck her. I opened the box and found a Spanish quaint edition of Lord of the Rings. There was a marking on a specific page, which was obviously the one where Galadriel gave the Fellowship of the Ring the gifts they would need for their travels. I laughed again, he had probably had to use Google Translate to find the right page. This time the lady changed seats. Good for her, I was very close to slipping a lorazepam in her coffee.

I kept inspecting the cardboard box. Deep at the bottom, I found a glass phial, which looked like it had held liquid medication until recently. The little bottle displayed a single violet flower in its core. Will had carefully thought all of it through, in such a way that almost made me feel something nice inside. There was also an envelope with 2000 dollars in cash, 200 euros in change, and countless tablets of lamotrigine, quetiapine, lorazepam and clonazepam. We hadn't found enough lorazepam to sustain me during my whole adventure, so I would have to settle for clonazepam. Beggars can't be choosers. I hugged the book and slept the whole way to Penn Station.

*   *   *

The sounds of the honks and sirens woke me up. For a split second, I thought I was back home, surrounded by the darkness of my room, with its endless recollection of memories and empty musings. But I awoke to a racket, a parade of flashing lights and the dancing echoes of this insomniac city. New York, still in mourning although it was 2005, was more alive than I had ever been.

It was 7.30 pm. I had just enough time to go shopping for some clothes before everything closed at 8. At least that's how it worked in dumbass Ohio. My mom would be wondering where I was by now, since I had left my phone back home, but Will had my full permission to give her cryptic messages about my whereabouts and my safety. Will didn't strike me as a mysterious, subtle guy, so he would probably blurt out the truth under my mom's first attempt at grilling him. He had made me promise to send him a postcard from every place I visited. I guessed it was his way of savoring the adventure he didn't dare live himself.

I entered a Kmart with a backpack full of money and a heart full of dreams. Bullshit, I just wanted to grab some clothes and get the hell out of that soppy place. I tossed a pair of $7 jeans inside the basket, $4 shorts, $2 leggings, a pack of six plain t-shirts for $11 (two white, two gray, two black, perfect), a $12 light jacket, a pack of 10 panties for $8 and a swimsuit for $10. I had planned on spending $60 max on my travel wear, but I needed a bag. And possibly a couple of bras. So the grand total was $82. Damn capitalism.

A falafel stand right around the corner of the Kmart was calling to me. It reminded me of that episode of *Friends*, when Rachel's sister thought Ross was the falafel guy. Maria, Philip and I would laugh our butts off with that TV show. We would sit for hours in Maria's sofa and play marathons of old seasons on DVD, eating popcorn, M&Ms and Snickers. The good ol' days. I probably looked like a retard reminiscing in the middle of the street, because the falafel guy called out to me to watch out.

"Thanks, my friend," I said. "Can I have a lamb one please, to go?" He nodded. "Cool turban, by the way."

The man looked up at me to check if I was mocking him. Topics related to Muslims were highly sensitive those days. And sadly, they would be forever. I assumed he saw the honesty in my face, because he offered me a complimentary beer, and who was I to turn down free booze?

As I made my way to a cyber café, I sipped my Budweiser and swallowed the falafel in one gulp. I was on a mission, there was no time to waste sightseeing or taking pics of the Madison Square Garden, as impressive and beautiful as the city was. I took a short stroll through the lively streets of Manhattan, until I chanced upon a 24-hour cyber café, where a bunch of nerds were pulling an all-nighter battling their dignity in a game of World of Warcraft. Just my kind of place.

I perched myself in the most recondite computer and started my search. I printed off maps and the address of my next destination. I felt a pang of guilt stab me in the mouth of my stomach, so I opened my Hotmail and sent my mom a brief e-mail. She'd be relieved to know I was still alive. Or quite the contrary, probably.

I then booked a flight to Europe for the following day. I could hear Will's obsessive voice reminding me to use the credit card for the big expenses, and cash and debit for the small ones. How had a guy who I had known for less than a month become the representative of my conscience? Damn his tedious neurosis. But I was a woman of my word...usually. So I grabbed the cheesiest postcard from the stall next to the cashier and wrote:

"Dear Statue of Willerty, I'm safe and sound. And almost sane. I'm off to Barcelona tomorrow afternoon. Insincerely, Lucy in the Skye. Monday June 21st 2005."

* * *

Damn it, damn it, DAMN IT! I could barely make the outlines of the human figures around me. My eyes were heavy with grogginess, both of my eyelids protruding unnaturally over my green eyes, which I bet were looking quite reddish at that moment. I tried to sit upright and immediately regretted it. Why did I have to smoke all that pot? There was a pool of vomit right next to my bag, decorating the already filthy floor of the Penn Station.

What damned time was it? I couldn't even make out the tiny numbers on my watch. I assumed it was morning, the station was bustling with the movement of early commuters. It had turned out that the geeks in the cyber café had an interesting stash of weed, and well, ignoring all sane warnings Will's voice of my conscience had given me, I had immersed myself in the world of marijuana, psychiatric medication, and lots and *lots* of beer. Now, I could hardly remember how I had found my way back to the station, let alone at what time I had to be at the airport.

"Are you okay there, girl?" a lady in a tight suit asked me with a disgusted face.

"Could you please tell me the time?" I answered blearily. She looked down at me, not in the least trying to pretend she wasn't revolted by me. "I'm not homeless or a junkie, ya know. Bitch!"

Well, that did it. She walked swiftly away, leaving a trail of stomping high heels and expensive perfume. Useless yuppie. I checked the big clock on the wall beside me, that should do it. If I couldn't see those numbers, then maybe I needed an ophthalmologist, not a shrink. It was 9.34am. If I remembered correctly, my flight left at 2.10pm, so I hurried to the ladies' room to make myself somewhat presentable before getting some breakfast.

I reeked. I knew I reeked. The people on the plane would just have to bear with me for eight hours. I tied my messy hair, washed my face and changed my shirt and trousers. There, as good as new. I was very much used to airports, having flown to Ireland countless times. I had a permit signed by both my parents allowing me to travel alone until I was 21, so that part was covered. Passports, covered too. Money, check. Bag with fairly decent clothes, check. The security guards didn't even look at me, they must have supposed I was a harmless, young woman, on my way to meet some fancy friends in Europe. They couldn't have been more wrong.

Lorazepam in hand, I boarded the plane. I was going to find my long lost dad, even if it took the life out of me.

CHAPTER FOUR

A BARGAIN FOR THE NUMBER TWO

*I*t was 4.30am when I hit the soil of Barcelona. I had never been to Spain before; the crisp air of this seaside city caressed my face with a welcoming touch. Buses were sparse at that time of the night, so I sat in an airport café until the first coach to the city departed at 6. I was wrecked, and I didn't long for my MIA father or even seeing a unicorn anymore, I just wanted a warm bed and a toothbrush.

The bus left me at *La Sagrada Familia*. Even with the scarce light of dawn, I was breath taken by its massive beauty. Half of the building was under construction, and even the monstrosity of nets, wires and ladders failed to mask the marvelous details of Gaudi's creation. I realized I was gaping with my mouth open, a face of awe this church must have been used to seeing.

I walked five or six blocks until I found the *"Regeneration Hostel"* I had marked on the map. Yay for me, super organized chick. Will would be proud. There was a teenage guy with an afro perched on the desk at the lobby, and he offered me a shared room with its own private bathroom. Anything would do. I knocked on the door to the large room on the third floor, carrying my bag all the way through the greasy staircase. A grumpy looking girl with tousled white blond hair opened up. I waved at her in thanks and tossed my bag in the only empty bed of the four bed room. After a quick shower, I put on my leggings, doped up, and gave in to a dreamless sleep.

*   *   *

Fourteen, FOURTEEN hours had passed when I woke up. It was 9.30pm, so I was awakened by the rumbling of my stomach. The room was empty, but I could hear the racket booming all the way from the ground floor. I had the nastiest migraine, and was unbearably jet-lagged, which did nothing for my mood. I put on my Kmart jean shorts and descended the three flight of stairs. I ordered a tuna sandwich and a diet Coke in the snack bar.

The lobby led into a vast area with a billiard table and a foosball board. The walls were lined with tacky red leather couches, where an Asian couple was very openly making out. There were some scattered tables with youngsters of all nationalities, given that the hair colors ranged from milky blond, like my roommate, to the darkest brown, matching the assortment of skins. I saw a tall, muscly guy give me an eye, and I immediately turned around, hoping for the love of god he wouldn't approach me.

"Hey *ginga*," he greeted me with the most annoying Australian accent, "care if I join you?"

"Go away," I answered, not even dignifying his presence with a look. I had glimpsed enough to see he was smoking hot, though. "I have bad breath. And I bite."

The Aussie laughed heartily. I wasn't being funny. "Irish, huh? I love the sense of humor you Lilliputians have up there."

Lilliputians? *Up there?* You are the one down *unda*, kangaroo. He was too hot to be even close to smart. "I don't speak English, sorry," I said in Spanish, while chewing on my sandwich. Very lady-like. Maybe my manly manners would scare him off?

"But I just heard you speak English!" Oh my God, he was impossibly thick. "I'm Nick." Nick the thick extended his tanned hand. I waved and left his hand hanging in midair. "So Irish then…"

"Nope."

"Oh! Canadian?"

"Nope."

"Hahaha! I like a challenge!" And I don't like you. "Don't tell me you are from Argentina…"

He managed to call my attention. "What made you think that?"

"The tattoo on your ankle! It's the Argentinian flag. I know my rugby teams," he affirmed proudly. 10 points for the dummy here. "Don't think I didn't check you out before coming over, ginger."

Just when it was going so well. "I'll tell you my name if you stop calling me ginger." I got up and busied myself with the leaflets in the rack by the snack bar. "Lucila."

"Nice to meet you, Luce." Oh boy, he had a talent for ruining the simplest things, even my name. "Would you fancy going out with me and some mates tonight?"

"Nah, sorry, I have nothing to wear, only my bad mood," I responded, quite truthfully, still busy with the leaflets for endless city tours and promises of novel, unique experiences. One of them caught my eye.

"But that can easily be solved, Luce!" he interjected happily. JUST GO AWAY MATE. "Oi, Annita! Come over here!" He waved at one of the many white blond girls slouching in the couches on the other side of the lobby.

A pair of endless legs responded to Nick's call. The legs were accompanied by a flawless body and a perfect face. Naturally. Standing next to Nick kangaroo, they looked like two models from those ridiculous perfume ads, where they frolic in a sea of petals, half-naked, and suddenly kiss for no reason over the background of the perfume brand.

"Hello, how are you? I'm Annita." Her accent was as strong as Nick's biceps. "You are my roommate, I think yes."

"Yeah, I think yes too," I joked, still enthralled by the pamphlet. "I'll tell you what Mick…"

"Nick," he corrected me, cheerfully of course.

"I'll go out with you and your *mates* if you take me here tomorrow." I pointed at the brochure.

"*The Ayahuasca Ritual*?" he asked surprised. "Sure, I'm game for anything. I'll have my mate Dave arrange it." He hadn't even read what it entailed. He probably couldn't even read more than three lines. "Now, for your end of the bargain, my friend Annita here," who he was very smoothly holding by her tiny waist, "will very generously lend you something to wear tonight."

Annita gave me a picture perfect smile. Grand, Miss Sweden's clothes would very likely make me look like a mantelpiece. Just my dream. We had to settle for one of Frida's, Swedish girl number 2, sleeveless tank tops. It was egg yolk yellow and had...ruffles. But she was the only one who was only 15cm taller than me. Swedish girl number 3, Julia, was at least 1.78m, and Annita was a skyscraper. They stuffed some cotton in a pair of Frida's flat boots, and handed me a brand new razor, even if I had pretty much no body hair. They probably didn't imagine my intimate past with razors, poor models, they had good intentions. They had no problem changing themselves in front of each other, but I chose to sneak into the bathroom for some privacy. They also lent me some make-up, which I applied scarcely, and finished the look with my Kmart black jacket, since it was very tiring to answer the stream of questions about my tattoos and various forms of scars. And there I was, a ginger borderline duckling, off into the endless possibilities of Barcelona's night.

* * *

When I opened my eyes, the first thing I noticed was that I was not alone, I was being...spooned. Squeezed, more than spooned, by a muscly, tanned arm. Oh my god, I remembered now, I had slept with Mick. Nick. Dick. Whatever. Flashes of a series of tequila shots and intoxicated moves at the beat of the Macarena also sparked in my groggy brain.

I gave the arm a hearty push, until I could get it off my body. I heard a dull thump as the knot of muscles fell sideways. I tiptoed until I found my jacket and Frida's boots on the floor...and just when

I thought I was safe to bail, I heard a sleepy voice whisper from the bed at the other end of the room. It was Nick's mate, Dave. "10.30 pm, lobby. See you there." I gave him a thumb up and slammed their door behind me.

CHAPTER FIVE

THE WISDOM OF THE FOUR AND THE ACCIDENTAL SEVEN

*A*t 10.30pm, my new girl pals, the trio of Swedes and I, met up with Dave (Nick's mate). Out of courtesy to me, or more likely out of hangover residues, Nick was a no show. But Dave had managed to rally a few Germans, a pair of very chirpy Brazilians, the loved-up Asian couple, with two huge cameras hanging from their necks, and a group of six loud, *loud* American jogs. I would definitely adopt my Irish identity around them, my Argentine identity just to piss off the Brazilian girls, and my American one the rest of the time. I didn't have a genuine identity, that is who I was, a big hole of nothingness, so pretending I was someone for real, at least for a little while, was a piece of cake.

We hopped on a bus from *La Sagrada Familia* to the base of Montjuic, an approximately 173m hill in the outskirts of Barcelona. The weather was soothingly mild, and I was grateful I had worn my shorts with my bikini under it. Hey, the pamphlet said "prepare of anything," so I assumed the wise way to go would be to wear a bikini and leave the money and the passports back at the hostel. We were greeted by an aboriginal looking man, who turned out to be Hugo, our shaman from Peru. He was wearing an irregular woolen tunic, in spite of the weather, with an embroidered Peruvian pattern. Beside him was Fermín, the local tour guide, whose English was a lot worse than my Spanish. And that is a lot to say. He had an untrimmed, whitish beard, which intertwined with the curly hairs of his chest. All courtesy of his open Hawaiian shirt.

They announced we would be climbing half a mile, until we reached the "ritual arena." We eventually found a clearing, amongst a breathtaking setting of short trees and tall bushes. There was a pile of logs in the center of the clearing, and small cushions forming a circle around it. Hugo and Fermín stood in the heart of the circle, and the rest of us sat in random positions. Fermín prompted us to introduce ourselves and explain the reasons why we were there. Maybe if I crouched really low, they wouldn't notice I was there but then my mane of red curls would give me away. Damn it, it was my turn.

"Hi everyone, my name is Lucy, and I am an addict," I joked, but nobody laughed. "I'm not an actual addict, don't worry." Serious faces still staring at me. This was harder than group therapy! "I'm here because…I'm bored." I shrugged. "Oh, and I would really like to see a unicorn, could you set that up for me?" I asked Hugo, who didn't respond.

When the rest of the group had finished their nonsensical blabbering, which I completely ignored, Fermín handed each one of us a wooden cup, while Hugo began to chant a hypnotic tune in an aboriginal language, shaking a wooden bottle at the rhythm of the chant. I was beginning to feel the dozing effects of the mantra, and by the time I had sipped the contents of the cup, I had already left this world.

I could faintly hear reverberations of retching sounds from afar. I felt a little nauseated myself, but I was overpowered by the numbness of my senses to focus on the nausea. My vision went blurry, a buzzing resonated in my ears, and a sour taste began to fill my mouth. I had to get away from that place. I stumbled through the bushes, scraping my bare legs, when the invading buzzing morphed into the echo of galloping hooves.

A horn, a purple horn, protruded from the bushes. Oh my god, it was a dazzling, fully-formed unicorn, staring back at me.

"Hop on, child," AND HE WAS SPEAKING, IN A HUMAN VOICE, "I will take you on a ride to your darkest nightmares and the confines of your deepest dreams."

"You are my dream, Centipede," I told him in what seemed like a faint echo of my childhood voice. "I have dreamt of you since I had my first Little Pony!"

"Come on child, we don't have all night," Centipede insisted. I jumped on his back and felt like was falling over a cascade of a million clouds. "I'll lead the way."

Centipede, the purple unicorn of my childhood dreams, drove me into the core the of the forest. The buzzing in my ears began to increase, depraving me from any sense of hearing. I didn't mind it as long as the night breeze kept stroking my face, and he was in control. And then I fell full face on to the ground. I didn't feel pain, just surprise as the unicorn nudged me with his horn to look around. He had tripped over a sea of bodies.

I gasped in horror. "They tried to cry for help, Lucy, but you just wouldn't listen," Centipede explained. I could make out the faces of my family on the forest's grass, Mom, Maria, Philip...all contorted in fear and agony. Tears of despair fell like waterfalls on my cheeks, but Centipede prompted me back on top of his mane.

"No, wait! I cannot leave them!" But my voice never took form. It was a mere whisper inside my head. Centipede kept galloping along the convoluted paths of the forest. I had recovered my hearing, but now I had lost my voice.

I could devise the outline of a figure running in front of us. As we approached the shadow, I started deciphering his features...tall, pale skin, unkempt mane of dark hair, glistening hazel eyes, wide open in desperation. It was Will.

"Centipede, STOP, we have to help Will! Please!" but no sound came out. Will kept running, glaring at me in despair, but his foot got tangled in a mess of branches and he was thrust into a hole in the ground. I tried to warn him, I tried to scream, but my lungs were gasping for the air that never managed to make my voice a concrete sound.

"Will tried to walk with you, but you just wouldn't speak Lucy. You only communicate with those who don't exist," enunciated the unicorn. He was a sage now?

"You don't know the first thing about me," I countered, this time out loud.

"How could I not? If I am you, Lucy." The unicorn turned around to face me, and that was the last thing I saw.

I could still feel the speed of his gape, the deafening rattle of the night forest, but my eyes were as dark as the sky above. We kept going until time no longer became a matter, and all that invaded me was a sickening smell of smoke.

"Fire Centipede, we are close to a fire!" I warned him. But he paid no heed. He tossed me to the ground, where I could feel the flames creeping up my skin.

"Centipede, get me back up, I can't see!"

"Child, you trapped yourself in this fire. Open your eyes and you'll see the light." With that, the unicorn was gone.

The sweltering fire was so unbearable I started ripping off my clothes. I was going to die, engulfed by a wolf of flames, and reduced into a forgettable heap of embers and ashes.

*   *   *

The sound of the sea awoke me. The sand grated my skin very unforgivably, and I had strands of algae in my hair. I was lying face down, my body in a contorted position, topless and barefoot. I saw the rest of my clothes close by. No one was around me. I brushed the sand off my skin, clothed in the speed of light, and found a cab back to the hostel, sobbing all the way for the dignity and the sanity that I would never recover.

CHAPTER SIX

THE PHILOSOPHY OF THE RAIN

It was 2.40am when I barged into my hostel room. Thankfully, the Swedes hadn't returned yet, and for the love of god, I hope they wouldn't any time soon. My mind was reeling with hallucinogenic flashes and the whirlwind of leftover emotions. I stormed into the bathroom and forced myself to vomit any residues of the ayahuasca concoction. I tossed all of my clothes into the basket and jumped into the shower, hoping the hot water, as long as it lasted, would cleanse me of my sins. I wasn't sure if all the water in the Iguazú Falls would do the deed.

I popped in my evening medication, which I had skipped, and tried to focus on the real, concrete things around me. My mind was a nasty mess of confusion and fear. Focus Lucy, focus. Come back to Earth. I spotted Annita's laptop on her bed, and to my fortune, it wasn't password protected and automatically connected to the hostel's wi fi. I checked my inbox, even though my eyes were finding it extraneously hard to see straight. 47 relevant e-mails. 44 from mom, 2 from Will and 1 from Maria. What had I done to them? What had I done to myself? I could have been kidnapped, raped, murdered. This mad behavior had to stop. I just didn't know how.

My heart started hammering against my slender chest, sweat dripping slowly down my forehead. My lungs were screaming for help. My brain began to broadcast a parade of horrific images, in consonance with the anxiety and guilt I was feeling. I was paralyzed, numb, confused…until the deafening sound of my own thoughts became the growing roar in my ears that yanked me from oblivion.

I ran into the bathroom and took my razor in my hands, as if I had just found a pot of gold at the end of the rainbow. The sharpness of its brand new edge was enticingly tempting, as was the piercing sensation it would cause against my recent wounds. The physical wounds anyway, the psychological ones were way past healing. They would remain raw and open for the rest of my life.

I knew cutting would give me instantaneous relief, like it had always done. It would calm my emotions at the synchronous pace it damaged my body. I knew just as well that it was no solution, that it was only a pathological, immature coping mechanism I would have to overcome eventually. But not now. The skin in my two wrists still looked pinkish and tender from my last suicide attempt, barely over 5 weeks back, and uncontrolled impulsiveness led me to stick the razor right in the angle of my left scar.

The popping sound of a new e-mail startled me. Who would write at this hour? I peered at Annita's laptop and saw it was Bruno. Right, it was 9 or 10pm in Cleveland. My heart skipped a beat, if something had happened to my family, that razor would go even deeper. I frantically opened the message, blood sliding over the bed's duvet.

"Lucy its Phil Daddy left the computer open I miss you come back soon"

This couldn't be happening. Philip, my 9-year-old cousin, had managed to find my e-mail address and urge me back home. I hit reply, knowing he would be expecting an immediate answer, before my uncle figured out his mischief.

"Hi big guy! I'm so sorry I left without saying goodbye, you know how your cousin goes a little whacky sometimes. I promise I will take care of myself, so that when I go back home, I can be a better cousin to you and Penny, a better daughter to auntie Olivia, and a better niece to auntie Maria and your daddy. Please be safe and have fun while I'm gone, I'll be back before you even know it. I love you, my big guy. Lucy."

The response appeared before I had time to wipe my tears.

"Lucy, it's Bruno. Sorry about that. I left my inbox open. Philip has been particularly naughty since you left. Reminds me of his big cousin. Lucy, your mother is inconsolable. We are all very concerned. Are you alright? Please come back home. Your family loves you no matter what. Uncle Bruno."

I lacked the strength to reply again. I slammed the computer shut and hurled the razor into the bathroom basket. I quickly put a Band-Aid on my wrist, chucked a lorazepam, and cried myself to sleep, hugging the pillow I wish was someone I knew and loved.

* * *

At 10.30am, the Swedes were sleeping peacefully. God, how I envied them. I was broken beyond repair, and with no medication to aid, sleep usually evaded me. With my stuff all packed, I checked out of the hostel and ventured into the Grácia neighborhood. I had decided overnight that I couldn't cope with the continuous rattle and comings and goings of the hostel, the people's prying and their obnoxious looks and intrusive questions. I needed to be alone and get back to the first stage of finding my dad.

Coming to Barcelona was based on the fact that his last letter had been posted from a Karate Dojo in the city, which address I had jotted down before coming on my trip. Very few letters and no photographs of my father were left in my possession. My mom had burned them all after he had written his unexplained farewell, but his goodbye postcard was one of the few I had been able to nick and save.

After walking a few blocks in the wrong direction, I found the Karate Dojo, together with a sign that announced that it was closed for the month of June, and would re-open Monday July 4th. Great, just great. I had ten days alone in Barcelona for exploring and self-reflection. I started by procuring me a room in one of the Onix Hotels, a cozy 2-star building that would more than suffice my needs. They were out of single rooms for the time being, so I was stuck in a double room with two beds, as if I needed another reminder of my loyal loneliness.

I left my bag and ate some lunch at one of those Michael Collins Irish Pubs. Maybe a good Irish Stew and a pint of Guinness, even with 30 degrees, would lift my spirits. Only one pint Lucy, I was on a path of moderation, normalcy and well-medicated self-control. Speaking of which, I kept my promise after I had finished my lunch, and sent a postcard to darling Will.

"Dear Sacred FamWilly, I might have lost my way, ever if I had one. I gave into my lower instincts with an Aussie dumbass, and caved into the temptation of some old vices and unhealthy habits. I never thought I would say this, but I might just need you to get here and kick my ass back on track. Insincerely, Lucy in the Skye. Thursday June 24th 2005"

After I had posted it, I was afraid he might take it seriously, so I popped him an e-mail from the hotel, ignoring the mounting unread ones in my inbox.

"Cadillac, when you get my Barcelona postcard, don't freak out, okay? I know it will be very much unlike you to stay calm, but chug a clonazepam if you have to. I guarantee you (and very possibly mom too) that I'm safe and sound in the Onix Hotel on Diagonal Avenue, you can check all the details online to see it's legit. I very much doubt you or mom will trust the value of my sacred word. But I even promise I'll try to stop the crazy acts for a few weeks. Lucy."

That should do it. Pleased with myself, I went to my room for a nap, smiling at the ridiculousness of the Spanish telenovelas. I woke up the next morning, my capacity to sleep on meds never ceased to astound me. I spent the day in a blur of touristic boredom, which wasn't a real challenge. I was always bored. And empty. I passed the time with some random shopping, I needed new clothes to add to my already scarce stock. Primark did the trick. I even purchased a floral dress I kept on, my first ever attempt to behave like everybody else.

The evening thunderstorm hit me while walking by the Rambla. Soaked and moody, I hurried back to the hotel. As much as I was used to the Irish dampness and crappy weather, having lived in Ireland for 8 years and spent my holidays there years after that, this was actual wet rain. A proper summer storm.

The rain made me miserable. It reminded of me of when my mom had told me the rain was God's way of showing us he was saddened by all the bad things humans did on Earth. It reminded me of Alfonsina Storni, the Argentine poet drowned in the sea. It reminded me of all the tears I had shed trying to understand why I was so different, and trying hard, but failing, at fitting in like the rest of the sheep. I would always be black, a dark soul, and empty hole of black and nothing.

I glimpsed at myself under the unforgiving elevator light. My curls had become a cluster of knots and tangles, and my new dress was sticking uncomfortably over my drenched skin. Thank god I was way past my "emo" phase, or I would have had to rub eyeliner off my cheeks all night long. I dropped the bags and screamed when I entered my room.

CHAPTER SEVEN

THE UNEXPECTED SIX

"*W*HAT-THE-*HELL*-ARE-*YOU*-DOING-HERE?!?" I yelled, running in rage towards the other end of the room.

"Happy to see me?" Will half-joked. He looked exhausted, frightened, relieved, and as sweet as ever. I squeezed him so hard that I started mistaking his breaths for mine, and his intoxicating smell of cologne began to numb me. He was a good two and a half heads taller than me, and he was leaning down over my hair. "I missed your curls," he whispered so softly the rumbling thunder almost covered it.

"Marry me." I kissed him savagely on the mouth.

"That was an unexpected reaction," he said grinning, his eyes so open I could see all the white around the hazel. I slapped him with the full force of my right hand. "Ouch. That's more like you," he responded this time, holding his cheek, but still grinning. I couldn't help but grin back.

"I have to go put some dry clothes on, you stay right where you are. You are only allowed to move to put on some hot water, Cadillac," I warned him, prodding a finger on his chest. "This will be a long night."

His response was muffled by the sound of the bathroom door, but I could still hear his soft chuckle, and something that had forever been hollow, suddenly felt solid.

*　*　*

"So you read my e-mail, thought I was in trouble, ran off to the airport and caught the earliest flight from Cleveland to Barcelona?" I repeated incredulously, blowing my hot tea. "And then I'm the insane one…"

Will blushed. The storm had subsided but had given into a slight drizzle that still echoed over the pavement. "What can I say, Skye. I don't know if it's magical, supernatural, or simply human, but you have a power over me." He shrugged, as if he had just given me the time.

"You won't win me over with cheap flattery, Cadillac," I lied, but I had that stupid feeling in my stomach of being on a plane while traveling through a bundle of clouds. "So I assume your well-off family paid for the tickets? And I assume my mom is aware of this impromptu trip of yours as well?"

"You assume correctly, twice," he responded, sipping his coffee. "And I'm not here to win you over with cheap flattery, you are better than that."

"You have a point. I am pretty awesome." I pointed out. "And poor little you too! You are so pathetic, and nervous, and stupid, and anxious and worried and uptight, and have such tinny-tiny self-esteem that you could never ever woo a girl, insane or otherwise. Right?" I put on an annoyingly childish voice, as I threw a pillow at him.

"We are *not* having a pillow fight, Dr. Skye," Will said, sending my pillow flying back to my bed. "And yes, exactly what you said. Add to that 22-year-old virgin with excessive sweating, insomnia and claustrophobia."

I laughed out loud. "Oh my god, I'm officially handing you over the trophy for worst nut job of the decade!" He did a curtsy. "All of those things can be easily fixed, Cadillac."

"Tell that to Dr. Whelan, she upped my dose of paroxetine, and wants to add Nozinan to the combo to help me sleep. Isn't that the stuff they give to old demented people?"

"Fuck her," I said, rolling my eyes. "Not literally, unless you are into old ladies and stuff." He grimaced. "Not that you would know, you could be gay for all we know, or asexual." He grimaced even harder. "Well, I guess there's only one way to find out, huh?"

Will looked taken aback. I jumped over him and kissed him again. Before we knew, clothes were off and love was on, with the music of the rain as our only witness.

*   *   *

It wasn't as if we held hands on the beach or gazed lovingly at each other's eyes. Will wouldn't let me touch his constantly sweaty hands anyway. It was about peace, silence, understanding, and company. Yes, of course we kissed, we went to the movies almost every day and laughed at the Spanish subtitles, we bathed in *La Barceloneta*, we even took the cableway above the skies of Barcelona, which turned out to backfire because Will had a claustrophobic panic attack. I had to hold his chest and remind him to breathe, and then buy him an ice-cream to improve his sour mood. The simplicity of men. So we talked, we shared with each other stories of our insanity, and sometimes we didn't have to talk at all.

He annoyed me endlessly. His stupid obsessiveness, his babysitting to check if I was taking my meds correctly, how he poured hot water into the mug before the tea bag! The way he dressed like he was ten years older and married to a soccer mom annoyed me. His tossing and turning at night annoyed me. His alarms set at the time for this tablets annoyed me. But the fact that *he* annoyed me, annoyed me the most.

"Hop in the shower with me, will ya?" I called out to him. It was Friday night and we were supposed to catch a late screening of Star Wars III: The Revenge of the Sith. "You'll never get over your damn self-esteem issues if you always hide your nakedness. It's not like you are *that* deformed!"

Will entered the bathroom swearing loudly at my cheekiness. "Okay, I'll get in with you if you promise to text your mom." I scoffed and quickly washed the conditioner off my curls. "She's been writing all week Skye, give her break."

"Perfect way to ruin the mood, Cadillac." I dried myself and left him alone in the bathroom to cower in his anxiety. I heard him turn on the shower, so I picked up his mobile and decided to send a brief message to my mother.

"*Hey Will! Are we still up for next week? XOXO.*" Who the fuck was Sarah? For his sake, she'd better be a therapist or a dentist or a reiki master, but not some *random* chick. I texted my mom and waited for Will to exit the bathroom, tossing his phone from one hand to another.

"Oh-oh, what did I do now?" He must have perceived my murderous frown.

"Nothing, as usual." I hurled the phone at him. "Sarah texted. She sends you hugs and kisses and wonders if you are still on for next week." What the hell was I doing? Had I become a regular, dim-witted, jealous chick?

"Oh boy," he sighed, shying away to a corner. "It's nothing, Skye. She's a girl from college I saw the other day after night class."

Oh no, damn it, the wrath had taken over. "A *girl?*"

"Yes Skye, and I'm a guy, so I asked her out," he tried to explain calmly, but sweat was sprinkling from his sideburns. "It honestly means nothing, she was nice, that's all."

"So what? Two days after I left, you just decided to ask a bitch out? What a gentleman you are," my voice was starting to take up a notch or two.

"We were just friends Lucy, and you *ran to Europe*! This is crazy!"

"Yes, because I'm so damn crazy, aren't I?" I was gesturing madly. "You know what your problem is, Cadillac? You lie to yourself. You think you are so amazing and daring and brave for having come save the crazy Borderline patient from her disasters. But all you want is normal. You want a boring, dull, regular life, with a *nice,* quiet bimbo to fix you dinner and ask you how your stupid day was!"

"And what if I want that?" he screamed. I had never seen him so angry. This was really bad. "Is it such a sin to want a happy life?" He started putting his clothes into his bag. "*You* are the one who is blind. Everyone pales in comparison next to you, Lucy. You are a shooting star, you are bright and special and fucking intense like nobody I've ever met in my dull, boring life. I've tread on muddy ground for 22 years, and this week, for the first time, I felt like I had a little bit of self-confidence, a little tiny bit of self-worth. And you had to go and ruin it with your senselessness!" He kept yelling and throwing his clothes in his bag. "I've always had my feet stuck in the mud, and you showed me the fucking sky."

"Just GREAT THEN, pack your things and leave, because that's always the solution for everyone, isn't it? Abandon me like everyone else does, because I'm so unstable and irrational! My mom has her precious job, my dad has his delusions, and now you scored yourself a date! So LEAVE, JUST GO AND LOOK FOR YOUR HAPPILY EVER AFTER WITH THAT STUPID BITCH IF THAT IS WHAT YOU WANT!"

Tears were streaming down both our faces. "I would have stayed with you, Lucy. I would have given up College, my savings, even my treatment for you. But this isn't right. You and I, we aren't right. Nobody wants to leave you…you just push everyone away." He sniffed and wiped his manly tears. "Goodbye Skye."

CHAPTER EIGHT

A BLAST FROM THE PAST

July 2005

The weekend scurried away amongst endless tears and useless moping around. I stayed in the hotel, sulking…I was angry, upset, lonely, guilty, sad, and mostly angry again. Sometimes all of them at once. It was a turmoil of feelings I could barely manage without resorting to alcohol, cutting or self-medication.

The Dojo opened on Monday at 9am. I forced down some breakfast at the hotel and swung by, hoping it would lead me to some long-awaited answers. The streets of Barcelona were awfully busy, and reaching the Dojo brought some welcomed silence.

"Good morning," I said in Spanish to the secretary at the front desk. She was in her mid-thirties, and had beautiful, dark skin and big, brown eyes. "I was wondering if I could speak to Sensei Siko."

She smiled amicably and replied in Spanish too, but I could detect a soft accent from somewhere else. "Good morning, how are you? Unfortunately, Sensei Siko is in Paraguay at the moment, giving a seminar on meditation."

My heart fell at my feet. "That sucks," I responded in English, and apologized. "Do you mind if I take a look around the place? I'm actually looking for someone else too."

"Sure, be my guest. The lessons don't start until 10."

A framed photograph hanging behind her desk caught my eye. A group of 20 or so people, all cloaked in karate attires or however they were called, were hugging and smiling at the camera. Two of them had bright, red hair and faces full of freckles.

"Excuse me, can I take a closer look at that picture?" She nodded and let me pass behind her chair. I traced my finger over the glass, trying to conjure with more clarity the memories I had of my father's features. His eyes and his voice were imprinted on my mind, but the details of his face were a washed out blur.

"Are you Irish?" the secretary asked softly. I turned around to face her, she seemed genuinely interested.

"Well, more or less. I was born in the US, but lived in Ireland for a good number of years," I explained. "My family on my mother's side is from Argentina. Sensei Siko should go there next, it's beautiful."

"I'll make sure to tell him." The secretary nodded. "I was born in Marrakesh, but moved to Barcelona when I was 18. I've been working here for 15 years, and I can't say that I've met anyone with your blood mixture."

"Lucky me," I said sourly, and turned back around to face the picture. She kept talking to me, why did she have to keep talking when I had to concentrate?

"The reason I asked is because those men you were looking at in the picture were Irish. And looked just like you, red hair, pale skin, short stature and all," she clarified, smiling. "Are you related to them?"

"I might be. Do you remember anything about them?" My heart was pounding frantically.

"To tell you the truth, they haven't been here in a while," she scratched her frizzy hair. "The youngest one was called Sean, the one on the right. I think he married his English girlfriend and moved to London a long time ago. That's when he stopped coming for the winter seminars. His brother continued coming, but we haven't seen him in quite a while. I can't seem to remember his name…"

"Alexander, perhaps?" I chanced.

"Exactly, yes!"

Alexander Skye was my father. I heard a bustle of people coming in through the front door, their noises nothing like the rattle in my own head. I had found a lead, and my new destination. I was going to find my uncle.

*　　*　　*

The plane landed in Heathrow Airport at 4.30pm on Wednesday July 6th. Excitement tickled every fiber of my body. The day before, I had researched my uncle online, and I had failed to procure an address or contact number. *But* he was a well-renown surgeon, currently medical director of one of the biggest general hospitals in London, so it wouldn't be hard to find. I hoped. I wished. I dreamed. I prayed. Not really prayed, I was an atheist, but you get the gist.

I had also booked a *single* room in another of the Onix Hotel chains, right next to King's Cross station. Having been to London many times as a little girl, I knew my way around the city, so I took a bus to the hotel and rested for the day. Thursday would be the beginning of a new chapter in my life.

I woke up at 7.30am, brimming with anticipation. I had never enjoyed cereal and milk so much. The plan for the day was to make some time around the area, then I would pop up by the hospital and find my uncle around noon, to maximize my chances of catching him on his lunch break. But I would crash the operating room if I had to, I was way beyond that point of dignity.

To my surprise, it wasn't raining, so I decided to take a walk along Travistock Park. Before I could stop myself, I was retrieving a postcard of the Big Ben from a souvenir shop and writing to Will.

"Dear Prince William of Cleveland, I can't apologize for who I am. I can't and I won't. But I can find the humility to apologize for behaving like a brat. I hope you and Sally have a wonderful date. Insincerely, Lucy in the Skye. Thursday July 7th, 2005." Short and sweet, untruthful, and posted in the mail.

It was the sour taste that filled my mouth what hit me first. For the space of a heartbeat, I thought it was jealousy and resentment over Will's date. But no, it was the iron flavor of blood. The piercing jab of the shattered glass on my face's skin followed. And then came the boom of the blast.

I still recall the events in slow motion. The deafening screams, the panic, the chaos, the smell of charred plastic and the ashes in my nostrils. Survival instinct made me ran, leaving everything behind, hoping only my legs, my heart, and my brain, wouldn't give in. I remember seeing a payphone, not knowing where I was, and dialing the only number I knew by heart, with the coins I still had in my pocket.

"Mom, mom! It's Lucy," I cried in desperation. I could barely hear my own voice with the roaring beep in my ears.

"Lucy, baby, oh my God! Are you okay? Where are you?" I could hear the despair in her voice, it was the middle of the night in Cleveland.

"I'm in London mom, and something terrible just happened. There was a bomb or something, I saw people dead on the street mom!" I was sobbing like a baby. "Mom, please, I'm so scared. I don't know what to do!"

She started crying uncontrollably, I could hear the TV in the background. "Oh my God Lucy, there's been a terrorist attack. Oh my God, oh my God. Lucy, listen to me," but I couldn't stop the shaking, the sheer terror running through my veins. "Get to a safe place. Oh my God," the despair in her voice made me want to vomit, "go to 1 Primrose Hill Road. Did you hear me Lucy? Are you still with me?" The line dropped before I could tell her I was sorry, and that I loved her more than anything in the world.

*   *   *

I don't remember getting in the taxi and arriving at that address. All I remember was the face of the woman who opened the door for me, the face of an angel, and fainting stone cold at her feet.

CHAPTER NINE

THE DREAMS I DREAM

*T*he sea was darker than usual. It had lost the crystalline sapphire quality of the Atlantic. Today it was petrol blue, in ominous warning of what was to come. I looked down at my hands and they seemed strangely small and fragile. I tried, to no use, to keep the ice-cream cone steady, but my arms lacked strength, they were limp and refusing to respond to my commands. The chocolate scoop landed first, leaving a dip in the sand. I was too drawn by the nostalgia of the loss to notice the gigantic wave towering above my body. Faint screams in the voice of my father tried to warn me, before I had to gasp for my last breath of air.

"Shit!" I yelled, bolting upright on the bed. I was soaked in sweat and my heart was in a frenzy.

I looked around to get my bearings. Right, I was in London. There had been a bombing. I had run to this house. I had slept for an entire day. The dim light of the morning filtered through the silk drapes, and I was dressed in classy pajamas. Everything in the room was fancy, I was deep in the most comfortable mattress I had ever been, and the sheets were as soft as cotton candy.

"Lucy, are you okay?" A lady asked from the other side of the oak door. "I thought I heard you scream."

"Yeah, come on in." It was the angel lady. "I'm fine," I lied. "But if you don't mind me asking, where the hell am I?"

The posh lady smiled empathically. She sat on the foot of the bed. "You are at your uncle Sean's house. I'm his wife, Camille DeMartini." I appreciated a lady who kept her last name. "You gave us quite the scare yesterday, landing like that on our doorstep!"

"Literally landing, huh." I sighed deeply. "That's the last thing I remember. What happened?"

"Well, as soon as you arrived I called your uncle. I knew who you were the minute I saw your face. You are the spitting image of your father, but unfortunately you take after your uncle's height," she joked. I liked her more by the minute. "Sean told me to call an ambulance and tell them to take you to his hospital. He arranged a CT scan and did some bloodwork, but you were fine, just in shock. They stitched up the side of your jaw and let you come home at night. The hospital was swamped with injured people from the bombings." Her tone was very low, and she had the poshest London accent.

"I don't remember any of it," I confessed, tracing a finger over the gash on my jaw. "Is Sean here now? I'd like to talk to him."

"I imagine you do," she said understandingly, "but he will be busy in theatre all day, with the tragedy that happened. He should be home by dinner."

The theatre? What? He was a surgeon by day, actor by night? Oh shit, the Brits called the operating room "theatre", right. Maybe I had hit my head with the blast.

"Can I call my mom? She'll be worried sick."

"Of course darling," Camille said. "You have a landline phone right there on your nightstand. Feel free to call whomever you want. I'll go fix breakfast and be back in a little while. You rest up."

It was 11am, 5 in the morning in Cleveland. But my mom probably hadn't slept at all anyway. She picked up right away.

"Hey Mammy, it's me," and the crying started.

"Oh my God Lucy, thank God!" Thank the doctors, mom, thank the doctors. "How are you baby?"

"I'm okay, I'm at Dad's brother's house."

"I know, Camille called me last night. She is a good woman," mom said amongst sobs.

"Why did you send me here anyway?" I tried to stand, but my whole body screamed in pain.

My mom sighed. "They are good people, and I remembered their address in London. They'll take care of you until I get there. I'm trying to book a flight, but it's impossible with everything that happened in the city!" She sounded desperate.

"Mom, I'm okay, honestly. I think I'm in good hands. Don't do anything rash, stay in Cleveland for the time being, okay? It might be dangerous to fly now." I sensed she wanted to argue my logic, but her presence would only complicate everything. And if something happened to her, I would blast the rest of London. "Don't be stupid, you should have learnt from your daughter by now not to engage in risky situations unnecessarily."

She laughed humorlessly. "I love you so much...you are my entire life Lucy."

I choked in tears, but managed to say, "I love you too mom, more than you know. I'll call you tonight. Take care," and hung up.

Goodness me, getting to the *en suite* bathroom was even harder than watching *Schindler's List*. I welcomed the warmth of the shower, the bathroom was massive and sparkled in marble. The fancy shampoo left a lavender fragrance in my hair, and I had to scrub off the residues of ashes and sweat three times with the expensive soap before feeling completely clean. I felt guilty for having smudged all those pretty sheets and pajamas, but it wasn't like this family couldn't replace them. There was a change of clothes neatly folded in the bathroom. I assumed they were some of Camille's old clothes. It was a long-sleeved black cotton dress and a red wool cardigan, with tiny flower buttons. Could have been worse.

Camille announced breakfast was ready, and asked me if I would like for her to bring me up a tray. I shouted back that I would be right down, I ached all over, but I wasn't a cripple. Although I could get used to the royalty treatment.

"Make yourself comfortable," Camille said, inviting me to the table. It had been hard enough to find the dining room in that mansion. "We don't really have assigned seats."

There was a guy a little older than me already me sitting at the table. He looked like a younger, and hairier, version of Jude Law. Hmmm, yummy. He waved at me as I took a seat.

"This is Marco, my son from a previous marriage," Camille explained as a black woman in an apron approached the table. "His father died when I was pregnant."

"I'm right here, mother," Marco snapped, eating his toast sulkily.

"You both met already, but you were very little, I doubt you remember," Camille continued, ignoring her son.

"Nice to re-meet you," I said distractedly, I was too focused on the lady coming and going bringing pastries, coffee and milk. "Oh my God, you have a maid!" I blurted out. I had never, *ever* seen anyone so freaking rich.

"I think you meant to say *slave*," Marco interjected, looking up for the first time. He had eyes the color of jade and tinge of gold in his skin. My infatuation was a little incestuous, but my step-cousin was drop dead gorgeous.

"Oh Marco, please don't start," Camille urged him in a whisper. "We have a guest, and she's been through a rough couple of days." Scratch that Camille, more like a rough couple of years.

"My apologies mother, I was just pointing out the truth."

"You will keep doing this even if I ask you not to, won't you?" Camille poured some coffee in my empty mug. "Sugar and cream Lucy, the American way?"

I nodded. I was more interested in their Wimbledon Final. I grabbed a croissant and continued watching. Was this what it was like when my mom and I argued during breakfast? I suddenly felt sorry for her.

"The hypocrisy we live in just upsets me," Marco resumed. "We eat bread and butter and bacon and toast and drink milk and coffee over some mindless chatter, when innocent animals are being slaughtered by the minute only to satisfy our greedy needs, not to mention people being enslaved and tortured under inhuman conditions."

Hey pal, you lost me there with your ramblings. I enjoy my bacon and love animals more than morning coffee at the same time.

"If this is about Mimi, I will tell you, *once again*, she has worked with us since she left Ethiopia, and is perfectly content. We treat her with respect and she earns a decent living." Camille was beginning to get flustered.

"Work *for* us, mother," Marco corrected. Camille slammed the table. She had a temper, I respected that.

"Stop it, Marco. You evidently fail to see that helping other comes in many ways. You don't have to be a doctor to help people Marco, Mimi is doing a dignified job that allowed her to put her two children in a good school. How is that slavery?"

"Does she eat with us?" Marco continued. Give it a rest pal. I really hoped Mimi wasn't eavesdropping on this conversation. I felt embarrassed for the rich kid. "It's asymmetry of power."

"Does a doctor eat with his patients? Does a politician eat with the citizens? Do I eat with my clients? It's not power, it's the role we are meant to play in this life."

"So, what do you guys do?" I interrupted them, Marco's arguments were making me sleepy. I chugged another croissant with butter.

"I'm a freelance Italian to English translator," Camille explained, putting on her charming smile again.

"Mamma mia!" I sang, and Camille laughed.

"Not like she needs to work, she just pretends to do something worthwhile because being a housewife is apparently *uncool*." Marco spat, still busy with his plain toast. Camille shifted uncomfortably in her chair.

"If you don't slap him, I will," I said with my mouth full. Camille laughed and Marco looked up in surprise. I bet he wasn't used to being told his place. "And what do you do, smart mouth?"

"I'm doing my Masters in Politics at King's College. Summer recess currently."

"Figures." I took a sip of my delicious coffee. "So when are you taking the private jet to party with your friends in Ibiza? Tonight or tomorrow? Or is it the Porsche to the north of France? And please, don't forget to take your Ray Bans and your Sony Ericsson, you might have a communist/vegan identity crisis over the holidays and no Mammy to make feel crappy about it."

With that, Mimi entered the room and cleared the table. She gave me the tiniest wink as she exited towards the kitchen.

* * *

Camille left me with Richie Rich to run some errands. Too bad I was in bed rest, I would have given anything to escape his pretentious company. He showed me to their spacious back yard, ordered by his mother.

"Whoa! Who lives there?" I asked, pointing at the loveliest wooden house by the back wall.

"Martin."

"For fuck sakes, you kidnapped a kid and have him trapped there? No wonder you are such a prick!"

"What on Earth are you going on about?" Marco looked disgusted at me. "Blimey, Martin is the dog!"

And just like that, the most beautiful Irish Russell Terrier surfaced from his house. Yes, the dog had a house. He came running to me so excitedly he knocked me down to the grass. I hadn't felt such happiness in days. There weren't many nice things one could highlight about me. I was a mess of a human being. But I *loved* dogs. Adored them. Worshipped them. They were the most pure, noble, loyal, perfect little angels. I just loved all animals with my whole hole of a black heart.

Martin kept licking my face despite Marco's warnings. Good boy Martin, ignore the brainless brat. I could have stayed all day just lying in the grass, frolicking like a child with the perfect dog. Mimi the maid appeared in the garden, asking what we wanted for lunch. Martin instantly looked up and jumped up to greet her. Oh boy, was he perfect. This day would have been okay if only Marco disappeared. Or simply stayed silent, I could work with that. And maybe if Will were there instead of Marco. STOP IT NOW, LUCY.

"A Caesar salad with no chicken for me Mimi, thank you," Marco said, looking at me to express my choice next.

"Ah…hi Mimi," I waved at her and smiled. "I'll have what everyone else is having, I guess." I shrugged and she smiled back. "Anything but salad, though." Mimi laughed and gave me a nod. She made her way into the house as Martin returned cheerfully to my arms.

* * *

This time, I was hanging on the edge of a cliff. Maybe it was a building's terrace, but there was a tsunami of waves below, eager to devour me. And, naturally, I dived to their midst.

I jolted awake, I had fallen straight asleep after dinner. My uncle Sean was still a no show. Martin, who was napping peacefully curled up in my legs, opened one eye and looked at me suspiciously. He decided he wouldn't be bothered by my nonsense and continued snoring. We both heard a soft knocking on the door.

"May I?" Camille asked, peeping her face through the door. Martin yawned and started wagging his tail at the sight of his mommy.

"Come on in, it's your house after all." Camille came in and left four bags on my bed. Martin hopped off the bed and Camille began rubbing his belly.

"I hope you don't mind, but I took the liberty of getting you some clothes. I know you lost your belongings in the bombings," she explained. Martin stuck his tongue into her mouth every time she spoke. "You are petite like me, so I assumed we'd be about the same size. You can change anything you want."

"Wow, thank you so much Camille, you really didn't have to."

I searched the bags for my new clothes, from *Zara*, *H&M*, *Benetton* and *Forever 21*. Not my typical go to places, I was more of a jeans and sneakers type of gal, but the clothes were very nice. Summer dresses, light pants, t-shirts, sweaters, flats, a backpack, even flip flops and a swimsuit. The colors ranged from soft pastels to bright patterns, it seemed she couldn't decide between what I would like and what would look good on me. There was a fifth bag from Boots with toiletries: tampons, cold wax, deodorant, comb, toothbrush, a vanilla hydrating cream, sunblock, and a very fancy *Cacharel* perfume. Whoa. I tried it on, a feminine and fruity fragrance filled my nostrils. I gave Camille a huge grin.

"Lucy, I need to ask you something." Martin sneezed at the smell of the perfume. "Your mother said something on the phone when we spoke…"

"Oh-oh, that's never good," I joked, petting Martin on his cute little head.

Camille smiled. "She mentioned you had some…troubles in the past, and that before coming here, you were under treatment." I averted her eyes, but nodded slightly. Big-mouthed mother of mine. "I was wondering if you wanted me to ask Sean for the tablets you lost. Olivia gave me the list."

I hesitated for a second. "Yeah whatever, okay." If my mom heard I had refused Camille's offer, she would flip out.

"Good," she said. "I was also wondering if you'd like Marco to accompany you to the American Embassy on Monday." I goggled at her. "I am very much aware he can be a bit of a headache sometimes…"

"Geez, he'd give Marx's corpse a headache."

"…but he is a good person, and he knows his way around the embassies. He even has some friends who can help speed up the process".

"Fine. But he'll have to take me to the Argentine and Irish embassies too, I lost all three passports."

"Sure." Camille was starting to get up, but seemed to change her mind. "And lastly…Sean called." My heart starting beating nervously, I was extremely anxious to see him and grill him on my dad's whereabouts. "He'll be working late today again, I'm so sorry." She must have seen the disappointment in my face. "I imagine how excited you must be to talk to him, that's why I thought tomorrow morning we could all take a weekend trip to Brighton. We have a beach house in a lovely, quiet spot. It'd be the perfect chance for you two to speak."

I liked the sound of that. "On one condition. We take Martin with us." The dog looked up at me cheerfully at the mention of his name. I could honestly eat him.

"Why of course, we always take our baby!" Camille exclaimed, and Martin resumed the tail wagging. The phone rang and Camille swiftly picked up. She looked at me.

"Lucy, it's for you." She gave me a wink and exited the room with Martin at her side.

"Hello?" I was expecting my mom, but a deep voice startled me. Dad?!?

"We watched *Space Jam* today, but it wasn't that much fun without you making snide comments in my ear." My heart began fluttering, damn it.

"You almost make me want to go back to Day Hospital, Cadillac." I was grinning so broadly my stitches stretched. Ouch.

"I wouldn't dream of it. How are you Lucy? Your mom gave me this number, I heard what happened."

"Not as good as you, I bet," I answered, dodging the question. "How was your date with Sally?"

Will puffed. "Sarah." I could almost picture him rolling his eyes. "It was nice."

"Did you sweat much?" I teased.

"Are you kidding me? I was a waterfall! I had to excuse myself three times to go dry my armpits."

I couldn't stop laughing. "Was it better than hanging out with a chick with Borderline Personality Disorder?"

"See? I don't think you fulfill the DSM-IV criteria for that," he responded, avoiding *my* question this time. "I rechecked it and you seem way wackier than that."

"I'm flattered," I said, laughing again. Gosh, I kind of missed him. I heard his aunt yelling something indistinct in the background.

"I have to go, Skye. Today was my last day at Day Hospital, and we're going out to celebrate."

"Wow, congratulations Cadillac. I'm so happy for you! Are you going back to College then?"

"On Monday, yeah, and I have weekly check-ups with Whelan." His voice changed into a softer tone. "I wish you were here."

I sighed. And I wish you were here. "I promise I'll dream of you tonight." I hung up the phone and wiped the tears off my face with the fancy pajamas.

I turned on the TV to get my mind off needing Will by my side. *Karate Kid* was on. Amazing, my favorite movie of all time. That night I dreamt of Will painting fences and me doing the crane stance behind him, both smiling at our matching insanities.

CHAPTER TEN

THE BEACH

*I*t was before 10am and I had already showered, packed for the weekend and changed. I had chosen a light green dress with a dark green sweater on top. Camille would be pleased to see I was wearing the clothes she had got for me, even if I looked like a deranged leprechaun. I even brushed my hair to make myself more presentable, this was a day for my history books.

"Good morning," Camille greeted me, but my heart had stopped at the sight of the back of a head full of red curls. A head which turned and was accompanied by a pair of small green eyes and a fully-freckled complexion. Sean stood up abruptly and gave me the truest, most candid and welcoming smile I had seen in my almost 21 years of life.

I considered myself quite the expert on Irish greetings. Having been brought up by a passionate Argentinean, I always laughed at the awkwardness of Irish personal contact. I had figured brief hugs and waves from afar were the best way to go with people with personal space issues, but Sean sprung up to me and embraced me for what felt like a sweet eternity.

"You've grown so much," my uncle said, assessing me from head to toe. He quickly examined my stitches. "How are you feeling?"

"Overwhelmed," I responded truthfully, "but okay." I sat down at the table next to him, Marco wasn't up yet.

"Isn't she beautiful?" Camille interjected, pouring me some coffee. I guessed Mimi worked from Monday to Friday. I twirled my head comically, and they both laughed.

"Hmmmm *pain au chocolat*!" I celebrated at the sight of my favorite pastry.

"Your Dad's favorite too," Sean said, clearly without thinking. And just when I thought that can of worms was open, Marco entered the room with a groggy face and messy hair, and the subject was dropped.

"Looks like you had fun last night," Camille chanced at Marco. Sean and I were still reeling from the sudden mention of my father.

"Same old, same old," Marco responded cryptically. We continued eating breakfast in an uncomfortable silence, with Martin licking my fingers underneath the table, until Camille announced it was time to hit the road.

For the two hours it took us to arrive to Brighton, Camille and I engulfed in an animated conversation about her Italian family, most of them still living in Piemonte, and the similarities between Italy and Argentina. After all, Argentineans, especially in the center of the country, are a rather special concoction between their Spanish and Italian heritage. The three males slept for almost the entire journey, Sean exhausted from his demands at work, Marco hungover and sleep deprived, and Martin knackered just by the simple fact of being a chipper dog. Their snores were a dissonant melody of disharmonic tunes and mismatched beats.

We arrived at the seaside town a little after noon. Camille parked their superb Mercedes Benz and we walked up to a fancy-looking restaurant in the marina. We ate a fishy lunch outside, with the sun shining shyly between the looming clouds. We then took a stroll along the Marine Parade up to the pier. Martin was panting with his tail half down, so we decided it was time to go to the Skye's house for a nap.

The house turned out to be a cozy three-bedroom building, with a short promenade that opened into a private beach, shared only by the neighborhood's owners. Camille led me into the downstairs bedroom, the guest room, with its own little bathroom and view to the outside. It was breathtakingly peaceful. Martin climbed the bed and made himself at home with me by his side, both of us falling quickly into an easy sleep.

I woke up with the sound of conversation. Camille and Sean were chatting in the kitchen, while she made tea and coffee. I waved at them as I surfaced from the guest room. Camille very unsubtly mentioned it was time for Martin's walk, and she disappeared into the garden with Martin jumping up and down behind her. Sean and I were finally alone. He averted my gaze until I could hold my breath no longer.

"We need to talk," I said decidedly, pouring myself a coffee. We sat across each other.

"I know, but I don't know where to start," Sean confessed, holding his face. He wasn't handsome, but he had a very kind face. "It has been so long…I feel like we barely know each other, for reasons that escape either of us." He still kept that Irish accent I loved so much.

"It wasn't our fault; it all fell apart when Dad left."

He assessed my face, as if he was seeing me again for the first time. "You look so much like him, and like your grandmother. You take after my height; I apologize about that." He sighed and looked away. "I can't say I wasn't surprised when I didn't see you at the funeral…"

My heart stopped. I grabbed my chest with both hands. "Oh my God, Sean, your mother died? I didn't know, Christ, I would have come!"

Sean looked like he was about to faint. "What? No Lucy! Your grandmother's fine." Had the Earth just lost its gravity? "I'm so sorry, I thought you knew!" He was shaking his head incredulously, pale as an egg white. "Oh my God Lucy, Alexander is gone."

I jumped from the table and slammed my back on the wall. "No, no, no…what do you mean *gone*? He's somewhere, out there, waiting for me…no, no…you're wrong!" I was crying desperately as he patted my hair. I fell to the floor.

"I'm so sorry Lucy, I'm so sorry..." my uncle kept whispering, rocking me in his arms. "I thought you knew, I'm so sorry...your dad killed himself four years ago."

*   *   *

The hazy bits and pieces would, fortunately, never come back to my memory. I had been later told by Camille I had done a lot of screaming, head banging, biting and scratching. I only recall the faint sound of the ambulance sirens, and waking up the following day with a sharp pang in both my buttocks. I had never had a psychomotor agitation before, and apparently, the emergency doctor was convinced I should be admitted, but Sean was unyielding to leave me in his care. He took full responsibility for my insanity and decided to avoid hospitalization. I was instead knocked out with an intramuscular sedative and an antipsychotic, and stayed under the close watch of my family. Even Marco stayed up to take a shift next to my unconscious body.

The following morning, Camille assisted me in taking a shower, since I had barely recovered from my comatose state. The hot water helped, but I was still very light-headed. While she prepared breakfast, I told her I was going for a walk with Martin to the beach. She looked very hesitant, but finally trusted me enough to let me wander alone a few meters away from the house. I buried my feet in the sand and stared at the waves, with Martin circling around me happily, oblivious to my pain. Or maybe he was just trying to cheer me up with his unconditional love, dogs are magical like that.

"May I join you?" a familiar voice asked.

"Come to babysit me?" I asked humorlessly. Marco sat next to me. He looked like an Adonis under the morning sun, his skin glowing with a gilded tinge.

"Definitely, it's an addictive hobby," he joked. "I actually came to say something."

"Marco, just as a friendly warning. Your communist blabber may do the trick and make me go all *Exorcist* on you."

He didn't laugh, naturally. "You are really hard to talk to, did you know?"

I nodded. "I have a friend who likes to remind me."

"Is that the bloke you keep going on about every five minutes?" Will, of course.

I shrugged, pretending not to know what he was implying. "Maybe." I resumed my doodling on the sand.

"Look Lucy, I know what you are going through."

"I doubt it..." I started saying, and Marco snapped.

"Shut the bloody hell up, for once! Let me speak." I rolled my eyes and signaled him to proceed. "I am very much aware my situation is different. My father died of a lymphoma when I wasn't even born, and my mom met Sean when I was two. So I pretty much had the love of a father, he took me in like I was his own." Marco sighed and paused for a moment. "But there's always been a part of me that just felt...scarred. Like an open wound that never managed to heal. It's a dull pain, an ache for not having met my real father...I think it's grief, Lucy."

"Yeah, I'll be feeling the power of grief for a long time too," I thought out loud.

"Yes, I know. Grief is a very powerful thing Lucy. It can destroy you. You either learn how to live with it and push it to a dark corner of yourself, or you let it take over and consume you."

"This is a very lame pep talk, Marco," I joked, and again, he didn't laugh.

"Not, it's not. It's a valuable life lesson your eldest cousin is trying to teach you," he responded seriously. "Don't be a smartass and hear me out. Don't let the grief take the better part of your life Lucy, face it and learn to cope with it. Otherwise, you are down the same path your father went through."

Tears started flowing down my eyes. "How do I fight it, Marco? I'm not strong enough."

He shrugged his shoulders. "I'm only 25, you know. But I think the recipe is to hold on to those you love."

I didn't even bother to dry my tears. I held Martin and asked, "will you take me to town, oh so wise cousin?" Marco nodded, standing swiftly up. "I need to send a postcard."

CHAPTER ELEVEN

A SKYE TYPE OF BIRTHDAY

*O*n Monday, Marco toured me around the Argentine, Irish and American embassies in London. They were crammed with people after the previous week's terrorist attacks, and most required an appointment. Thankfully, Marco worked his magic and pulled some strings to get me seen in the three embassies, with the corresponding three promises of having my passports ready by the end of the week. And he must have had the right friends, because I had the three documents sent to the Skye's house by Friday.

The week passed me by in a wisp, because despite my pain, life kept moving forward. I had mostly overcome the shock of learning about my father's death, and the first few days were mainly a battle between sadness and complete fury. My mom called me every day twice, and even if I refused to speak to her at first for having withheld the truth from me for so long, I eventually gave in and let her hear my voice, if only in monosyllables. At least I found comfort in knowing that the following stages of grief would be the solace of denial and the long desired acceptance.

The only respite amongst that sea of misery were the nightly conversations with Will, and oddly enough, the daily walks with Martin and Mimi. We would take Martin out every morning to Primrose Hill. Most of the time Mimi remained silent, unless I asked her questions about her home country or her family. She was a very well-mannered, soft-spoken woman, and every word she uttered was filled with a wisdom I hoped I'd attain one day. When in pain, one can find friendship in the most unexpected of places.

It was Saturday July 16th at 11.45pm, 15 minutes shy of my 21st birthday. Mimi had been kind enough to come over for dinner with her husband, Donald, and their two daughters, Iris, 16, and Sophia, 14. I'm sure the food was wonderful, to me it was a mass of insipid cardboard I had to force down my throat. We started opening my presents in the living room, you could almost taste the affection in the room, except I was a hollow cave of grief and anger.

Mimi gave me, on behalf of his family, a rectangular box. Inside, she had carefully placed a dazzling small pendant in the form of a spiky cross, with an intricate pattern and embroidered with sparkling stones. It was hanging from a thin, silver chain. It wasn't an expensive jewel, its value was far from material, it was her thoughtfulness that made it a unique piece. I was moved when she explained it was the Coptic Cross, a symbol of her religion, and she was giving it to me as a talisman of faith. *"I hope this reminds you that don't need to believe in God to have faith, my dear,"* she whispered in my ear as we hugged. And the cryfest began.

Next was Marco. His box was a lot bigger and had the *Nike* logo printed all over it. So much for surprise presents. He had bought me a pair of fancy black trainers.

"I remember you said you missed your disgusting runners, so I thought this might help. My mother told me your size," he explained, and I gave him a smile and a quick hug. I did like running away from things, he was right about that.

Camille was overly excited for me to open her present. The heavy box was wrapped in shiny paper and soon I discovered it was a brand new super modern *HP* laptop. Leave it to Camille to fly right over the top. I was flabbergasted, and Camille mistook my silence. Martin was busy nibbling on the fallen wrapping paper.

"Oh Lucy, we can exchange it for something else if you don't like it. But you can video chat with your mom and Will now," she began explaining frantically. "And look," she turned on the computer, "we scanned and uploaded all the pictures of you and your Dad we could find. Turns out we had quite a few in our old family albums." I was still dead silent. I couldn't find the strength to speak. "Marco helped..."

"I almost had to chop off your cheeks to fit the photos in the scanner, you were one fat baby. Look at the broomstick you are now!" he joked, and we all laughed. Camille was still looking at me expectantly, and I jumped to hold her in a tight embrace. She was a wonderful woman.

"Speaking of which," Camille said, and I picked up the cryptic tone. "This came in the mail the other day."

She handed me a large FedEx box. I tore it open, it was full of birthday cards from my twin cousins, Maria and my mom. I would cry my eyes out reading them later in the solitude of my room. There was also a red leather wallet. I peered inside and it held 1000 dollars. I knew that was my mom, worried because I had lost all the money in the bombings. Mothers will be mothers. I felt a haul in my grieving heart.

At the bottom of the box, there was a large envelope. I knew it was from Will. That, I didn't dare open in front of everyone else, so I just kept it there, grabbed the rest of my presents, and announced I'd be going up to my room to put them away safely.

"Wait!" Camille interrupted me, "we still have to eat the cake Mimi baked."

"And I have to give you my present," Sean whispered in my ear, giving me the slightest of winks.

They sang me "Happy Birthday" and I pretended to enjoy it. The cake was a lovely chocolate sponge filled with caramel and topped with merengue. Marco was thrilled Mimi and her family had joined us in the celebrations, and he wouldn't stop pestering them to engage in conversation. When we finished the cake, Mimi and her family left, and Marco and Camille left Sean and I alone for a while, at his request.

"Lucy," he began, holding my hand. "I don't think there's anything I can give you that will make up for the lost years...or that will prove how much I, and mainly your dad, truly loved you." Salty water in the form of pearls began caressing my cheeks and filling my mouth. Sean gave me a rusty looking book, with yellowed pages and cracked borders. "Your father was a very sick man, doctors finally concluded he was Bipolar…but in all his…*madness*, there were bright moments of brilliance and creativity." He pointed at the book. "That's when he wrote this book of short stories, 10 years ago, a little after he decided it was safer for you if he wasn't around." I started choking in my tears. "My parents have one copy, and I want you to have the only other one, in hope it will bring some light to that darkness that haunts you."

Next thing I knew, he was cradling me in his arms; he was cradling a ball of raw emotions and bleeding wounds.

*   *   *

We hopped on the taxi and made a few turns until we reached the trendy club. Loud music was booming from inside, and a large queue occupied most of the block. Marco had insisted that I joined him and his College friends on a night out, even if all I wanted was to hide myself in the loneliness of my tears. We met with Paul, Daniel, Christian, Carla, Brenda and Andrea. Or maybe it was Paula, Daniella, Christina, Carl, Brendan and Andrew. I couldn't care less. I would avoid calling them by their names all night and that was that.

Of course we skipped the queue, these rich kids of London had their connections. They were all very keen on me trying the master bartender's drinks, but I had decided I would stay away from alcoholic beverages, for all the good it had done all these years…one of Marco's friends kept eyeing me annoyingly, like he wanted to establish some sort of eye contact that would evolve into making out and maybe something else. Ew, I was in mourning.

Around 2am, when my genocidal instincts were at its peak, this guy, let's name him Andrew, asked me if I wanted to join him outside, since he was going for a smoke. I craved for some fresh air, so I very stupidly agreed. I don't know what was more annoying, if his stinking breath of alcohol or his mindless small talk in that insufferable accent. I saw him pop a couple of pills, which I very much doubted were Tic Tacs. He offered me some, promising they would take me on a "trip of a lifetime." Definitely not Tic Tacs. No, thank you Andrew, I had already embarked upon one of those and it wasn't going so well.

Before I knew it, he was pinning me against the club's back wall, trying to stick his tongue in my mouth. He overpowered me in height and strength, his pants were already half down, and he was tugging on my dress to pull it upwards, his other hand on my throat. My heart started pounding hysterically, and my brain summoned my mom's frown, saying "*if a guy ever tries to hurt you, you just kick him in the nuts.*" And so, for the first time in my life, I followed my mom's advice.

When Marco came looking for me, I was gasping for air against the wall, and Andrew was on the floor grabbing his groin and swearing very un-elegantly at me. I yelled at Marco in a croaked voice to get a taxi, and inebriated as my cousin was, he managed to find one quickly and take me back home.

"So sorry Lucy," Marco blabbered, his tongue slugging under the effect of the booze. "Andrew had never done that…creep, taking advantage of a woman, female oppression drives me insane…let's go to the police Lucy…"

"Men are pigs Marco, my deepest apologies to pigs," I coughed, rolling my eyes. "Alcohol and ecstasy only make their primal instincts within resurface." Did I really believe that about all men or was it rage and fear speaking? "Shut up now, your breath and your ramblings are making me sick." The taxi driver eyed us suspiciously and soon left us at the Skye's house.

Back in my room, I jumped in the shower to cleanse my skin off the stench of cigarette and human depravity. I traced my finger over the envelope Will had sent me, unsure if I had the strength to face the secrets it held inside. Martin was already curled on my pillow, and I perched next to him, the envelope tight in my chest. I opened the seal and took a deep breath.

"Dear Skye, I don't think I'll ever find the words to express properly what I want to say. I would have gone over them a thousand times and still not be satisfied. You know my obsessiveness. I thought a drawing might convey them more properly. Beware, I'm more of a technical drawer, so please don't laugh at it. I hope it helps you understand the way I imagine your world. Lucy in her world, Lucy in the Skye. Love, Will."

It was a landscape drawing of a girl, sitting on the edge of the world. I could see the back of her curly, red hair and her green dress. She was staring at the starry universe, a large moon illuminating her figure. On the left side of picture, there was a purple unicorn flying away from the moon, and a set of stars scintillating all around it. The girl had her arm wrapped around a small dog; a tiny glass bottle with a single violet in its core hanging from his collar. Both of them were sitting in the front seat of a convertible car, a Cadillac parked on the edge of the world with them.

I have no idea why, but I started laughing madly. An incontrollable, deeply relieving bout of laughter. Martin started wagging his tail in surprise. Stupid, dumbass Will! When I was done laughing, I picked up the phone. It was only a little after 9.30pm in Cleveland. Will picked up after a couple of rings.

"You, me, video chat. Add me to Skype, lucy_skye. See you in a bit." And I hung up.

Half an hour later, Will popped up in my new laptop's screen. God, I hated him so much.

"Skye! What the heck do you think you are doing? I was supposed to call you first thing tomorrow to wish you Happy Birthday," he complained, with the hugest grin on his face.

"Nice to see you too, asshole," I answered back, failing at suppressing the grin on my own face. "I wanted to thank you 'personally' for that wacky drawing you sent me."

He blushed a little. "Only fair to draw something ridiculous for a ridiculous person like you. I mean, who else dreams of flying unicorns?"

"Ohhh trust me, I've seen one, and I'm not planning on riding that train again any time soon," I said, petting Martin, who had fallen back asleep.

"I don't think I wanna know," Will scoffed. "Are you okay Skye?"

"Well," I sighed, "considering we broke up before even getting together, I survived a terrorist attack, then found out my dad offed himself four years ago and everyone knew but me, and now a guy tried to assault me…I'm quite fine."

"WHAT?!?" Will jumped from his chair. "A guy tried to assault you? Did you report him? I'm going to find his sorry ass and fucking kill him!"

"Calm down, Robin Hood. He's one of Marco's prick friends. He was drunk and had taken ecstasy I think, I'm sure my big cousin will take care of it." Will was still punching his fist. "I wish you were here."

"So do I," he said in a low voice. Did he just lower his laptop's volume? "I miss your curls."

"I can tell, they were quite over the top in that drawing of yours," I joked. "And hey, wanna meet the other protagonist of the drawing?" I held Martin's sleepy body to the camera. Will started laughing.

"Oh my God, he's gorgeous Skye, no wonder you keep gushing about him," Will said, and started speaking to Martin in the most annoying baby voice. Martin wagged his tail a little and then fell asleep on my lap. Dogs, so wonderfully simple. Just like men. The good men, at least. "You'd better kidnap him and bring him to Cleveland when you come back home."

Will's door slammed open. I saw a blond head peering inside his room. "Get back out here, Willy, we miss ya!"

"Be right there," Will answered. All the blood had rushed to his face. "Sorry about that."

"Was that Sally? Does she have a southern accent?" I asked with disgust. "Please tell me I'm wrong."

"Sarah, yeah, she's from New Orleans," he responded, clearing his throat.

"Ugh Cadillac…so how's the family introduction going?" He had replaced me with a southern belle?

"Do you really want to talk about it?"

"No."

"So…back to the previous topic," he shifted in his chair uncomfortably. "When are you coming back home?"

"I *am* going home, Cadillac," I responded, ready to close the video chat window. "I'm going to Ireland."

CHAPTER TWELVE

THE OVEN LIFE

*W*hy is it that the sky looks so different from above than from below? A mass of menacing clouds and convoluted strikes of light surrounded the plane, while safe from the bosom of the land, innocent eyes must have seen nothing but a peaceful grayish mantle. Is that what happens with people? Are we a tornado of lightning and a tempest inside, but do we all seem composed, serene and collected from a distance?

After my video chat with Will, I had booked the earliest flight to Dublin. I had left the Skye's house barely after 5am, before anyone was up, I couldn't bear to say goodbye. I was a fragile knot of wrath and sadness. I had left Martin sleeping deeply in what had been my bed for the past ten days, and then scribbled a note for the family. My family.

"Dear all, you have made me feel loved and understood like never before, you have shown me the true meaning of family. Don't think I'm leaving because I don't appreciate that, I just need answers to questions that, probably, shouldn't even be asked. Love and a million thank you, Lucy."

The plane landed smoothly in Dublin despite the gathering storm. It was a little after 8am, so I had a quick breakfast and took the Airlink to Heuston station. There was a train to Galway departing at 10.15am, with an estimated arrival at 12.25am. Perfect, I would have the whole afternoon of my birthday to sulk alone in my gloomy desolation. The train left the station a few minutes late, and I felt that familiar poke at my heart that meant I was back home. Ireland was my home, with its endless imperfections, its laid-back, careless people, its messy disorganization and its loving, nurturing nature, that oozed from every pore of every being, shamrock and wave.

I was soon enthralled by the blooming landscape. I hadn't been in Ireland in ten years, and despite having lived there almost half my life, its beauty never ceased to amaze me. The countryside opened into an infinite valley of emerald hills and scattered sheep adorning them like cotton, interrupted only by the running streams, gleaming under the hazy Irish Sun. Sleep found me hastily, and when I woke up, we were close to Galway.

I walked for half an hour, all the way from the station to Doctor Colohan Road, I remembered distinctly the bungalow in Salthill where my Dad took me every summer. I didn't care if it was now occupied by a happy Ingalls family, that place would always be ours. I knocked on the door, my heart beating frantically, and I was almost knocked to the floor an instant later.

"For the love of Jaysus!" shouted an old lady with curly, gray hair and a tiny, sturdy frame. She reminded me of…Sean. My heart went from beating manically to slowing down to a full stop. She held her chest and then pinched my cheeks. "We haven't seen you in Donkey's years, my darling! Come on in, come on in, I'll put the kettle on. Aidan, wake up ya eejit, our granddaughter's here!" And that was Tilly, my grandmother.

I stepped into the house and, immediately, a black wiener dog came running up to me, barking madly and wagging her tail, equally as mad. She jumped up and down my leg, until I gave her my full attention.

"Hey," I responded shyly to Tilly, who I didn't even remember. I held the dog to hide my embarrassment.

"Look at the state o' ya, Lucy," Tilly complained, assessing me from head to toe. "You're thinner than a stack of rashers! Did you even have lunch?" I shook my head and laughed out loud at Tilly's outraged face.

"Ah, the cheek o' ya, old hag, lay off the poor girl," Aidan screamed from his rocking chair. His accent was so thick I could barely make out what he was saying. My grandfather had a pristine white Maltese dog perched beside him, who looked just as wise and grumpy as Aidan did. The dog didn't even bother to leave the chair when I went to greet them, he moved his curled tail slightly and gave me a quick lick. "He likes you," Aidan said, winking an eye at me, and then hugged me briefly. "This is so unexpected. Welcome home, Lucy."

"I love animals," I responded, still in shock, at loss for the right words. The wiener dog was twisting like crazy in my arms. I placed my backpack on the couch.

"Ah well, this is King," Aidan explained, pointing at the royal looking Maltese, "and that in your arms is Charlie, short for bloody bonkers sausage Charlotte." She soared from my arms to Aidan's lap, and King growled impatiently. Charlie was hyperactive, and bloody bonkers, for sure.

"How d'ya like yer eggs, Lucy?" Tilly asked from the kitchen, which was connected to the main living area.

"Whatever's fine," I answered, and I heard Tilly puff in complete scandal. A dark brown, furry cat descended the stairs, yawning carelessly.

"And that is Poppy," Aidan said a little too loudly, "the evil mastermind of the house. Mind that one, she's a ninja champ." Poppy glanced at me, uninterested, until I reached out to her and caressed her fluffy neck. Gotcha, little spawn of the devil. She purred softly and bumped her head into my hand. Charlie came running back, jealous of the attention Poppy was suddenly getting. I was in Animal Heaven!

"Lunch is ready," Tilly announced a few minutes later, and she shoved a plate full of scrambled eggs, bacon, sausage and beans on the table. "This is usually what we have for breakfast, but with yer size, I assumed it'd be more than enough."

"Thanks Tilly," I said, and she looked at me like she was about to slap me.

"Grandma to you, missy," she corrected me, pointing a chubby finger at my face. She was terrifying. "And don't think I don't know what day it is today either. July 17th, the birth of my only granddaughter. Happy birthday, darling. You showing up here today made me feel alive again." She gave me a peck on the cheek and wiped her tears as she put a cake dough in the oven.

*   *   *

The book was called "*The 8 Ways to Go Mad*." The 8 was lopsided, like the sign representing the infinite. The Infinite Ways to Go Mad. Suitable name for the author. My Dad had written eight fantasy/horror stories about madness, his topic of preference, just like mine. I started with the first one, "The Room for Uncertainty", and instantly fell in love with every word he had written. Every phrase, every character, every plot twist, was a step closer to finding out about his lost soul. And about mine in turn.

Tilly had made me call my mom and Sean. My mom was used to my bouts of craziness by now, but she was still relieved to hear I was safe and sound. Maria was with her, and it was lovely to hear her voice singing "Happy Birthday" to me, as if nothing had happened. Sean was a little bit more taken aback to hear I had landed in his motherland, but having had a Bipolar brother, I don't think he was that surprised. Camille had also wanted to speak to me.

My mom made me promise I would get a cell phone immediately, and that I'd call her every day. Nobody understood what I was doing there, but good for them, I didn't understand what I was doing with my life at all. My mother had sworn never to speak about my father to me after he left us, and had forbidden all of his family to contact me. I hated her for it, so much, even if she had done it to protect me. I kept punishing her for denying me that side of my life, over and over and over again.

There was so much about Alexander Skye that was still a mystery to me. I needed to know who he was, who he had been. All I remembered about my father was that he was an English teacher with a bright smile and piercing green eyes. I fell asleep in my old room with the book in my hands and Charlie next to me. Apparently, I was a magnet for dogs as much as I was for madness. I didn't even have time to brood in nostalgia, exhaustion caught up with me first. And thank god it did, because at 7am sharp, Tilly woke me up.

"Time for breakfast, Lucy," she called out from the downstairs floor. Charlie hurled herself from the bed, and Poppy, who had very slickly sneaked into my room in the middle of the night, yawned at me lazily from the foot of the bed. I descended in my pajamas with the cat behind me.

"Top o' the mornin' to ya," I said to Tilly, in a very fake Irish accent.

"You do know that's a shite phrase Hollywood made up," she pointed out, as she served breakfast. Aidan was nowhere to be seen. "Yer grandfather likes to sleep in, that lazy gobshite. Retirement doesn't suit 'im."

Tilly went on to elaborate on their story. Aidan was a retired History teacher, and she had worked her whole life at the bakery she had inherited from her mother, "*Sweet Booth*", down in town. She had closed it after my father's death, but it was obvious it was a topic she didn't want to delve in. Tilly now ran a very small catering company from the house, where they had also moved in after my dad's suicide. She only had one employee, but she had quite evidently devised a plan to acquire a second one.

"This looks very yummy," I said, chugging a piece of French toast.

"Yes, and you will learn how to make it, in time." The toast got caught in my throat.

"I can't cook," I explained, throwing the rest of the toast to an expectant Charlie. I had suddenly lost my appetite.

"As long as you live here, you, Lucy, will be my new apprentice," Tilly retorted, pointing her chubby finger at me, in that bossy way she fancied so much. "Eoin McHugh, that witless brat of an assistant

I have, will be here at noon to introduce you to the wonders of this wee company I like to call '*ChanTilly*'."

I cleared my throat. "Okay grandma." Maybe Tilly had turned my dad into her apprentice too and that's why he had offed himself. It all made sense now.

"And you will finish that breakfast, don't think I didn't see you drop that toast under the table, you brat." She filled my plate with homemade pastries. "You will be up every day at 7, you will take your tablets and, after breakfast, I will teach you how to whisk, roll, chop, grate, mix, melt, stir, shake, flake and bake."

"That'd be a cool rap song."

Tilly ignored me purposely and snapped her fingers to help me refocus. "In the afternoon, you will run the errands for the company, and every night I will give you a lesson on gourmet cooking." I nodded, suddenly reminded of the infinite ways to go mad. "But this morning we will do some shopping in town. You need an apron, your own cooking tools and utensils, a couple of jumpers for this fierce weather. Oh, and that mobile shite I promised your mam. Understood?"

"Sir, yes, sir." I gave her an army salutation and she hid a smile very poorly in response.

*   *   *

"Eoin," I started, and he interrupted me already.

"It's pronounced like 'Owen'."

"Whatever, Eowyn has more charm, like the kickass Rohan princess that kills the Witch-king of Angmar because he mistakes her for a man. Stupid asshole," I insisted, disregarding Eoin completely. "We will get along as you stay out of my business and put up with my bullshit. In turn, I'll pretend to pay attention to what you say and fake politeness."

"Phew, you take after your grandma, alright!" He laughed heartily.

"I'll take that as a compliment."

We were heading to one of Tilly's client's houses. On the way, Eoin explained he was training to be a chef in a local college. He had classes in the afternoon this semester, so I was now in charge of doing the shopping for Tilly's catering and going to the prospective clients' houses to take down their orders. He would help us every morning to get the orders ready, but I would have to deliver the ones scheduled for the afternoons and evenings. How had my father killed himself? I was thinking sticking my head inside one of Tilly's ovens would be a poetic way to get my message across.

After a few weeks had passed, I had gotten used to the hectic rhythm of Tilly's company, and I had even managed to bake a platter of *pain au chocolats*, without burning them. That was a first. Cooking was strangely therapeutic, as was being constantly surrounded by two caring grandparents and their three mad pets. Being across the sea also had a calming effect, and I was so tired at night that I barely had time to indulge in my typical self-loathing. I had sparks of moments when I even enjoyed myself.

So pumped I was by this injection of healthy energy, that one August night, I decided to go for a walk on the beach, exhausted by the week's labors. I didn't know what it was to feel happy, content, fulfilled, satisfied. I thought that was it, I thought that just like that, busy with a new craft and close to my father's death, I was complete. Immensely foolish like I was, endlessly immature, eternally idiotic, I tossed the lamotrigine, the quetiapine and the lorazepam one by one to the sea.

"Some whale will have a good craic getting high tonight," I said out loud, using the Irish slang and feeling proud of my stupid decision, like I usually was. "Just don't tell Marco fishy fishes, or he'll go all Greenpeace on me."

And, of course, it all went downhill from there.

CHAPTER THIRTEEN

NUMBER EIGHT WITH A TWIST

September 2005

t was a cool September morning when I first noticed something was seriously wrong. It had started with the return of the mood swings, mainly towards a downward pit. Then came the urge to self-harm, the blue tinge of the fire from the kitchen stoves began to look particularly tempting. Later on, the hushed whispers formed in my mind and lowered to my ears, surreptitiously escalating into fully formed voices.

"Normal" people usually believe us "crazies" can't tell when our crazy is back. Most of us, even during the worst of times, still have insight. I remember perfectly well the day I tried to kill myself for the first time. I was 16 and had just lost my virginity to a high school schmuck. My mom had found out and given me the reprimand of my life, I always felt she refrained from slapping me that day. I knew for a fact she thought I was a whore, that I was no use failing school, drinking, talking to imaginary voices, dyeing my hair, tattooing my body and cutting my skin. Or maybe that's how *I* felt, and not her. I don't know, I never asked her, but the emotions were so overwhelming, the frustration so suffocating, that all I could do was sneak into the medication cabinet and take it all in to take it all out.

In retrospect, maybe all I wanted was peace. The day I slit my wrists in May, earlier that year, we had fought over me going to college. What was a 20-year-old doing slacking around the house all day? I was a good for nothing creep, and all I was good at was at doing nothing. I didn't even cut the veins right. But then again, maybe I didn't want to die, maybe all I wanted was peace.

And peace I wanted again. I didn't know at that point how my father had killed himself, nobody dared tell me, I suspected in fear I would mimic his behavior. Normal people don't really know how to talk to us, how to approach us, I reckon they feel that if they say something wrong, we will take a gun and start shooting. They don't understand that our pain is ours and ours alone, and we don't wish to inflict it on anyone else, but only to our faulty selves. Because that pain, sometimes, is the only thing that reminds us we are still alive.

But when that pain turns unbearable, the minds starts to wonder, and then it begins to wander. It gets lost in the tortured musings of sadness and confusion, and in its most vulnerable state, when it should stop and ask for help, sometimes it retreats and follows the suggestions of the ill-advised voices, leading to what I've baptized "the point of no return."

I knew I was a coward. I knew that all I did was, unintentionally mostly, hurt the people I loved. I knew I was selfish and weak and that I had no reason to feel worthless. I knew I had so much to live for, and I knew I could survive this, like I had, so many times before. What I didn't know was if I wanted to. I had the knowledge, I just didn't have the will.

"You look knackered, Lucy," said Tilly, eyeing me suspiciously. "How do you feel in yourself at the moment?"

"I'm feeling a little under the weather," I lied, and she scrutinized me even more closely.

"Are you taking your meds?" she asked, and I busied myself with the oven to hide the lies.

"Yeah."

"Then why have you been acting so strange lately? Look at me when I'm talking to you, young lady," she commanded me in an authoritative voice. "You have been barking at your mam louder than Charlie, and that poor Will lad has been bombarded as well. Even your half-deaf grandfather hears your bickering."

"And you are half-witless, ye witch," grandpa shouted from their room. I turned scarlet.

It was the end of the summer, and we had tons of cakes to get ready for the last of the seasonal weddings. I was breaking some eggs following Tilly's orders, but she had other priorities in mind.

"Lucy dear, I raised a boy who was lovely and smart and charming and perfect to me in every possible way. Your father was just like you, so much more than you imagine." Tilly cupped my chin and stared deep into my eyes. "But he was also sensitive and vulnerable and stubborn and he just…felt too much. I lost him to his mind, and to the troubles of his soul."

I dropped the eggs and started crying relentlessly. "I'm in so much pain, grandma. I'm finding it hard to breathe."

"I know. We all do sometimes." Tilly sat down at the table. "I still feel like half my heart was ripped out of me the day your father died. I still feel lonely, and incomplete, even when this house is bustling with guests, even when I'm walking down a street full of people." She took a deep breath and held both my hands. "We are all flawed, Lucy, we all have our secret struggles and our more or less crazy shenanigans. So a little crazy won't scare this old hag. You can talk to me."

Tilly wiped a tear off my cheek. "I feel so helpless, and so, so alone."

"Alex wasn't alone, and neither are you, as long as you remember you are loved and that your life means something to those who love you. Don't ever forget that. You will find purpose in living when you understand that your life has meaning to you too. But that will only come the day you learn to love yourself, perfectly imperfect as you are."

"Thank you, grandma." I blew my nose with a napkin. Charlie kept bringing me all her squeaky toys and dirty socks from my laundry basket to cheer me up. She finally settled with stealing the nasty napkin. She was the most persistent, perky, precious thing, and

I loved her dearly. "It's curious, a couple of months ago, Marco gave me a similar speech about love and loss."

"Ah, good man, that one. Fair play to him," said my grandma pointing at herself. "He must have learnt a few good lessons from his step grandmother. Although I can't say he doesn't have some kind of crazy himself, even if he's not on the meds and such."

I laughed softly. "Do you mind if I take the day off? Eoin will be here by 10."

"Yer a lot better than the lad at decorating the cakes…but feck it, I'm sure it'll be grand." I dried the rest of tears with the back of the apron. "Be back by dinner and don't do anything I wouldn't do," she threatened, flicking her favorite chubby finger. I hugged her tightly and set off to the cliffs.

*   *   *

An hour and a half after I had hopped on the bus, I arrived at the Cliffs of Moher in County Clare. The "Terrible Beauty" of the Wild Atlantic Way. Erected majestically at almost 215m on their highest point, they stretched for 8km until they slowly transformed into low slopes opening to the ocean. It was a lovely, clear Wednesday of the last day of Summer, and Galway Bay and the Aran Islands could be outlined from afar. I knew in my heart that my dad had jumped precisely from that spot.

I had left most of my belongings back at the bungalow. To be completely honest, I had no clue as to what I was really doing there. The cliffs wouldn't speak to me in the way I'd have liked them to. I walked for a couple of hours, and when my legs protested in pain, I sat in a remote corner, away from the clutter of tourists. I retrieved a pen and the Galway postcard from my bag.

"Dear Willysses by James Joyce, I'm currently sitting at the edge of life, very much like you drew me. You know my favorite author said 'not all who wander are lost'. Well, I'm wandering along the footsteps of my Dad's last journey, lost in his path of insanity. Is that what awaits me? The same fate of desolation and loneliness? You gave me hope amidst my void. I'll

never stop wishing you were here, with me, shining your light into my
senseless dark. I'll dream of you, Lucy. September 21ˢᵗ 2005."

I tucked the postcard back into the bag and took my Dad's book instead. There was a short story about being trapped in an island encircled by a never ending abyss, entitled "The Mind Island". I was desperate to find answers, to understand his desperation, to comprehend the absurdity of his final choice. But the absurd has no answers, only more intricate puzzles of irrational interrogations.

A white butterfly flew past me, imposing with her outstretched wings and shining pallor. If she wasn't afraid of her imminent death, if she was courageous and splendid in what could be her last flight, why was I? I stood entranced by her swirling endeavor into the bottom of the slope, and just like a wingless butterfly, gravity betrayed me, and I plunged 13 meters into my death, still embracing my father's words.

CHAPTER FOURTEEN

GOODBYE SKYE

November 2005

This time, the unfamiliar chill awoke me. It is very hard to get your bearings when you have been doped up for several weeks. At least I assumed I had been in hospital for a considerable time, but my memory was still a cloud of haze and IV medication. My eyes complained at the brightness of the pristine hospital room. Okay, everything was clean and smelled good, so I wasn't in a Psych institution. Not yet at least.

I turned my head slowly to my left side. My arm and entire leg were in casts, I was wearing a sort of corset in my chest, I had a harness in my hip, and tubes of all sizes sticking out of several parts of my body...nose, veins in the arm, chest, belly...and other holes. My right side was bandaged, and so was my forehead, as far as I could detect. My hand was wrapped around a bracelet that read "Galway Central Hospital". My throat felt even sorer than my bones, so I pressed a red buzzer in my hand to call for a nurse. I craved water as much as a dose of morphine.

"SHE'S AWAKE, SHE'S AWAKE!" a familiar voice screeched from the hallway. My always so calm mother, Olivia. She barged into the room with her siblings, Maria and Bruno, by her side, yelling desperately for a doctor, who to my fortune, came quickly enough to refill my morphine and put me to sleep again. It was the morning of Saturday November 26th 2005 when I opened my eyes for the first time.

Later that evening, I reawakened. I was conscious enough to see all the people outside the room, sitting and standing expectantly in the hallway. All the people I loved. Mom was deep in conversation with my grandma Tilly, my aunt Maria had my little cousin Phillip on her lap, and Bruno, his dad, was caressing his hair. Phil was playing with a game console. Penelope and my aunt Greta must have had a life or death fourth grade spelling bee and couldn't make it to Ireland, surely. Next to my mother's family, were Sean and Camille speaking hurriedly to a doctor; Mimi, her husband and Marco slouched on the seats behind them. And in the far, far corner, was a gangly, nervous looking young man holding a coffee, beautiful in his clot of anxiety and kindness, the warmth of his heart reaching out across the hall.

"Will," I croaked, and as if he had magically heard me, he looked up and beamed at me. He crossed a few words with my family and the doctor, blushing desperately from his neck to his forehead, but finally entered my room.

"Nice way to spend your Saturday night, Skye," he greeted me, and I reached out my right hand to him.

"Your girlfriend must be missing your sweaty palms," I teased back, but they were dry when he held me.

"You know you scared me shitless, right?" He squeezed my hand and pulled a chair closer to my bed. "I hope you scared yourself shitless too, crazy piece of red curls."

I smiled. "They must be looking crazier than ever."

"Don't fret, they match your bloodshot eyes and your bleeding lips," he responded, grinning helplessly.

"How long was I out?" I attempted to sit upright, like the usual fool I was.

"Stay put, dumbass, you were in a coma for six weeks!" Will pushed me gently back down. "They brought you to a common room three weeks ago, you were breathing on your own, but you have a broken arm, three broken ribs, a broken hip, a broken femur, in three pieces I might add, and a completely shattered shin. Apparently, you landed on your left side on a bush over the sand. You missed the rocks by inches."

"Lucky me." I rolled my eyes.

"The doctors said you would be awake around this time, that's when most of us flew in to Galway. Your mom was so distraught; she was here from day one, she wouldn't leave your side, even in ICU."

"For fuck sakes, poor mom."

"Oh, they had to stitch up your left kidney and you had a pulmonary contusion. You almost lost your spleen too. And you'll have a scar on your forehead forever."

"Well, it'll match the ones inside!" I attempted to joke, but Will remained serious.

"What the hell did you do, Skye?" He clasped my hand even tighter. I couldn't lie to Will. Not to Will.

"I slipped," I confessed, holding his gaze. "I don't remember anything from that day, but I *know* I didn't jump Will."

"I knew it, I knew it," he whispered, shaking his head. "They found your backpack up on the hill and your mom gave me your last postcard. Everyone thinks you jumped, but I knew they were wrong."

I stared into the haven of his hazel eyes. "And let them continue to believe that, please." He opened his eyes widely and let go of my hand. "Listen to me, Cadillac. It's high time I stopped behaving like a mindless bitch. I can't go on like this," he started to argue, but I shut him up. "I've been trapped in a coil of selfishness and self-loathing for 21 years. I'm not a child anymore, I can't keep destroying everything I touch." Tears began to form in my eyes, mirroring Will's. "The only way I will grow out if this is if I receive proper help. I can't do that in Cleveland, with my family so close, watching over me." I looked outside, everyone still cheering and grinning simply because I was alive. What had I done to deserve them? "I need to stay, however long it takes, and heal. Here," I pointed at my heart, "and here," I raised my finger to my head.

Will sighed and stayed deep in thought for a long pause. "Fine, Skye. I can't say I like it, but I know how you feel, better than you think. I know what it's like to fight a monster inside every day, trying to control it and failing every time. I know that constant struggle."

"Thank you, Will."

"So, you will need this more than I thought." He fetched a thick book from his backpack, his favorite, Edgar Allan Poe's compilation of tales.

"Awww, marry me!" I half-joked, smiling innocently.

He looked at my hand and held it again. "Ha-ha…I suppose I can't, now that I'm really engaged," he said sheepishly, still staring at my hand.

"Oh, Christ." I gulped and choked a little. The smile had been suddenly wiped off my face. "But you are 22," was all I could muster to say, coughing stupidly.

"23 in March, and we will wait for another year to get married, probably," he explained, still not daring to look into my eyes. "We really bonded with Sarah when I traveled with her to New Orleans after Katrina. She was wrecked, and well, one thing led to another…"

Poor Will, always sacrificing himself for the happiness of others. "Congratulations are in order then, I'm happy for both of you," I lied terribly, letting go of his hand and taking a sip of water. "Wow, look at all that people gathered outside, queuing to see me. I'm the main act of the night," I continued lightly, to ease the awkwardness. "You should go, Will." He looked up at me this time, a crease had formed in his forehead as he frowned in pain. "You should go home."

I knew he was deeply hurt, but he took it like the decent man he was and nodded briefly. He grabbed his backpack again and retrieved a large glass bottle with the most stunning collection of violet petals inside. He left it on the hospital room's nightstand, before saying, "goodbye Skye," and not looking back once.

*   *   *

"Mom, mom, just breathe." My mother was making a scandal in the middle of the room. Maria was patting her back. "Sean has arranged everything for me to be transferred to Saint John's University Hospital, a psychiatric hospital in Dublin. He'll take care of the medical bills." She started to wave frantically in protest. "I will get the best care there, and I'll call you every single day."

It was a week before Christmas and I was almost ready to be released into the loving care of the doctors of the mind. I would have to continue daily physiotherapy there and weekly GP check-ups, but I would be fit enough for transfer soon. "You are completely delusional if you think I'm going back to the States without you!" Olivia grabbed her cheeks and pulled her hair dramatically.

"Oli, maybe you should listen to Lucy," Maria interjected, always the mediating voice. "She has a point, you know. We have to go back to work, and we will do no good just hovering around here. She has to figure out this independently, as the young woman she is."

"I won't abandon my child like her father did!" Mom was pacing up and down the room, still tugging at her silky black hair. Even in distress she looked stunning and radiated a blinding light.

"Mom, please, you are giving me a headache," and a heartache. "We will spend Christmas and New Year's together, and after that, you have to promise you will go back to Cleveland. My transfer is scheduled for Monday January 2nd, and that's that. I'm putting my broken foot down."

"If you miss ONE single call, I swear to you, and I SWEAR child," my mother yelled, "that I will take a private jet and drag you from your hair back home!"

"Cross my heart," I agreed, and aunt Maria smiled. "Now scamper off and bring me a *pain au chocolat* from O'Brien's before I bite your head off."

They left swiftly, and I was left alone to gloat in what had been my first ever selfless act.

CHAPTER FIFTEEN

THE START OF NUMBER TEN

January 2006

ow. I had toured around Ireland as a little girl, so I was used to the marvel of the Medieval castles. But I had never seen a hospital look so magnificent in my life, and boy did I know about Psychiatric Institutions. This was a massive, stone building, surrounded by a width of bushy trees and perfectly trimmed assortments of flowers, forming natural paths towards the hospital's entrance. I even spotted a squirrel scampering up one of the emerald canopies, and I couldn't help but feel the charm of the place.

My room was on the third floor, all the lounge areas and therapy rooms on the floor had an open view to a couple of tennis courts, an immense golf course and the Dublin Bay just a few meters behind. It was breathtaking. On the second floor, there was a roofed pool, a gym, a kitchen for occupational therapy purposes and an art room decorated with the works of the patients. The carpeted hallways of the ground floor were lightened by large chandeliers and lined with classrooms for the many medical students and psychiatry trainees bustling around the premises. And to top it all, the common dining room for patients was a circular glass palace that emanated the sensation of a warm greenhouse, and there were even three menu options to choose from! *Daaaamn.*

My roommate's name was Choi; she was a sweet local Dubliner, around my age. This was her third admission for depression and agoraphobia. She was the one who showed me around and introduced me to other veteran patients. We were on a women's ward, but we had some relative freedom to wander through the common places. I had a schedule to follow, of course, but this hospital had more staff than I had imagined. I had been admitted by a nice Psych trainee, Dr. Deirdre "overtired" Clark, whom I saw every morning for the typical "are you sleeping, eating, hearing voices, having suicidal thoughts?" assessment.

I was briefly evaluated on the first day by Dr. Something Murphy, the consultant (or attending, as we called them in the US). He made some appearances during the ward rounds, but he barely spoke to me. Arsehole. And then I had Dialectic Behavioral Therapy on Tuesdays with a group therapist and other enchanting Borderlines. Every afternoon after lunch, I had a physiotherapy session, and my personal favorite were Wednesdays of Occupational Therapy, where we could actually learn some useful skills.

The GP came once a week to examine me, he was particularly keen on knowing if I had coughed, spat, peed, pooped or remotely seen blood anywhere close to my body. He also did a neurological exam every time he visited, which was always normal, as the scans had showed. At least the macroscopic structure of my head was preserved. My wounds were healing adequately and he put me on a nutrition plan to start regaining some lost weight. He also switched me from codeine to something less potent, which did little for my pain, but at least wouldn't turn me into a toothless, hairless, scabious junkie.

"Come on in, please," said my appointed psychiatrist. It was the Friday of the third week since I had been admitted. The doctor was sitting at a comfortable looking couch in one of the therapy rooms. Her hair was shiny, dark brown, and styled in a bob with a fringe. Her skin was even paler than mine, and shone under the light that filtered through the large window. Her eyes were blue like the sea behind, and her teeth were a perfect assortment of white pearls. She looked like a stunning porcelain doll. Ugh. "I'm Dr. J.M. Carroll, pleasure to meet you."

"And I'm your current crazy Borderline to torture," I said in return, slouching in a similar couch opposite her. J.M. couldn't have been over 30.

"I think I prefer Lucy, is that what you like to be called?" She had a posh South Dublin accent, that wasn't completely hard on the ears. I nodded briefly. "Good." She gave me a kind smile, God, was she obnoxious. "Lucy, first things first, this will be a space and a time you and I will both share. So there is one basic rule, mutual respect. The moment that line is crossed, this space, and this time, are over."

"Maybe I want it to be over before it even starts," I muttered.

"Then you just have to say the word and we will both find something more useful to do. But there's no need to be disrespectful."

"Do you always give this introductory speech?"

She smiled again, she seemed unnerved by my defiant attitude. "Only to the people I think might need it."

"Oh, so Psych stands for psychic."

"It stands for Psychiatrist, I'm a medical doctor and a Senior Registrar in this hospital. You will see your Psychologist on Tuesdays and your psychic on your time off, you'd do well to remember that."

"Is that rule number two?"

"Sure, I usually make them up along the sessions," J.M. confessed. "Rule number three then. You will stop lying to the medical students. The Psychiatry Lecturer came up to me yesterday and complained. You will please stop telling them you are a hermaphrodite or that you think the CIA is after you or any made up nonsense of the sort. One day, those students might find themselves in a position where they can help you, but now, you are the one who can help them. So do it properly or shut up, but don't mess with their education."

"Oh, geez, sorry, I didn't think it was such a big deal." I shrugged.

"So what do you usually think about?" my psychiatrist asked.

"For instance, I thought this chat would be about my meds, not a sermon."

"It will be about your medication, definitely, when it is necessary to talk about it. Otherwise, it is not the only topic we will deal with. I am also interested in your thoughts, emotions and behaviors, and I hope you are too." I shrugged again as if I was 12. "Was there something in particular you wanted to mention about your medication scheme?"

"I feel drowsy in the mornings and I still find it hard to fall asleep."

"Okay, let me see," she quickly checked my chart. "You've been back on the lamotrigine, the quetiapine and the lorazepam for three weeks now, but you had been off them for a couple of months, as I understand. You know it's normal to feel sleepy the first few weeks, but I'll change your morning lorazepam to the night so that you are more awake during the day and rest better at night. Would that suit?"

"Aren't you the one who's supposed to know?"

"I have seven years of experience, psychiatric qualifications in three countries and a degree in psychotherapy. But I'm not the one taking the tablets. If you don't tell me what you think or how you feel, I'll have to guess. These are your body and your mind, not mine. And back to second rule, I'm not a psychic."

"Touché. Okay then, lorazepam all at night it is."

She jotted down something on the chart and signed it. "Anything else bugging you?" You.

"No," I lied. Fuck you.

"Are you swearing at me?" She grinned broadly.

"Jesus! I thought you sucked at guessing," and we both laughed. "You are quite annoying, lady."

"Likewise, lady," she responded, still laughing. "I think I know why *you* find *me* annoying. You sit there having to listen to my rules and my lectures, probably feeling you are better off gazing at the sea while you feel sorry for yourself and hate on the world, correct?"

"Spot on."

"Right. Is that why you come across as so 'annoying'?"

"Don't take it personally, I'm like that with everyone."

"Why?"

"I don't know."

She sighed. "Rule number four, is it? *I don't know* is not valid here. I will press you on until we are both satisfied with your answer."

"Shit," I snapped. "Oops, sorry, the respect thing."

"Swearing is allowed as long as it's controlled. We are not changing who you are. But violence and aggression are never allowed."

"I'm not good at control, I have Borderline Personality Disorder, you should know that," I defied her again.

"Ugh, I hate labels. They will call you 'Emotionally Unstable' here. You are not a tag to me, this isn't a supermarket. You are a person, I am a person, and we are having a conversation that I hope is in some way productive. So, why do you give the impression of being annoying?"

"I don't think about it, I just do it."

"Is that usually the way you behave?"

"Yeah."

"Have you always been like that?"

"Pretty much."

"Why?"

"I don't know."

"Try again."

"Fuck you." I pretended to cover my mouth in regret. "If people stay away, they can't hurt me. Isn't that a pathetic cliché or what?"

"Is that what you really think?"

"Yeah."

"So, basically, after your father left, you started pushing people away to avoid them hurting you. So you lose them before having them to avoid losing them?"

"How screwed up is that?!?" We both chuckled.

"Terribly, Lucy," she joked. "What happens when you feel hurt?"

"Oh boy…I go to the extreme. I choke, I scream, I cry, I cut my arms, I drink, I flea, I self-medicate or lay off the pills at all, whatever it takes to numb myself."

"Then, as you said, in your own words, you have an issue with extremes and control. Objective number one, learn to find balance. Control your impulses. Put a rein on your urges."

"Do we have to number the objectives too? I forgot about the rules already."

"So did I, that's why I take notes. You can do the same if you like. Do you enjoy writing?"

"I have no idea."

"What do you enjoy doing?"

"I'm good at nothing," I barfed.

"Show me evidence or else your statement is invalid."

"I didn't even go to college J.M., how can I be good at something?"

"Lucy, prove that nonsense wrong. Tell me what you enjoy and what you are good at."

I pondered her question for a moment. "I…like cooking. I helped my grandma with her catering company for a little while." J.M nodded and smiled, saying nothing. "I also like taking care of pets, I have a soft spot for animals."

"Excellent. Both activities entail a lot of love. Good for you," she said honestly, and I was pleasantly surprised. "You might not be so bad then."

We laughed. "I'm horrible J.M…that's why I'm here, I've been acting like a spoiled, selfish, immature girl my whole life."

"And that's why you are here?"

"Yes, I couldn't keep doing this to my family, to my friend Will…"

"Why?"

"It wasn't fair on them."

"Why?" Shit, I was already crying.

"Because they care about me, and I care about them."

"So, you are full of love. Love for cooking, love for animals, love for your family. Is there any sort of love you are missing?"

"Do you mean like a boyfriend?"

"No."

"I don't know then."

"Try again."

"Ahhhh!" I screamed, she drove me even crazier than I was.

"You are annoying, useless, worthless, and emotionally unstable. How can we destroy those misconceptions?"

"Loving my fucking self?"

"Loving your fucking self indeed."

"Are you sure you are psychiatrist?" I probed.

"Are you sure you are crazy?" she challenged back, and we laughed together again. Damn her, this was worse than my hour at the gym with the physiotherapist.

"Objective number two, learn to love myself?"

"Objective number two, challenge and replace your learned behaviors and automatic thoughts by new, most positive concepts. Valuing your self-worth is one of them. Do you think you can do that?"

"If you tell me how."

"Practice, and me being very annoying."

"Even more?!?!" I teased.

"Oh Lucy, we haven't even started," she half-joked. "I'll give you assignments every week." She looked at the time. "It's almost noon, so we are about to finish. Your assignment for next week is to cook me and the other patients on your ward *empanadas de pollo* during your OT kitchen session."

"What the fuck?" Her Spanish was better than mine!

"You heard me correctly," J.M. insisted, "chicken empanadas are my favorite."

"Alright, I guess." She stood up grinning and showed me to the door. I stopped and sized her up from head to toe. She was at least two heads taller than I was, and very graceful.

"Wait, what does J.M. stand for?"

"Juana Martina," my doctor responded, opening the door. "Irish father and Argentine mother...what are the odds?" She winked and eye and led me out.

CHAPTER SIXTEEN

MENTAL WORKOUT BURNS CALORIES

"Close your eyes and picture this situation," J.M. started at the beginning of our session. "You are 21 years old, your parents are together living in Ireland, and your father leaves a postcard and disappears. How do you react?"

"I chase him around the world until I find him and kick his ass."

"Do you think of the immediate consequences of your decision before taking it?"

"No."

"Do you consider how the rest of the people who you love you might feel?"

"No."

"Do you pause to ponder the pros and cons of your decision?"

"No."

"Do you think about the long-term effects your decision might have on you and your loved ones?"

"No."

"Do you take a moment to outweigh the negative impact of your decision over the instantaneous relief it might give you?"

"No."

"Do you consider an alternative?"

"No."

"Open your eyes please," J.M. commanded. "Do you find anything wrong or modifiable in from what you learnt in this exercise?"

"I probably should have said 'yes' to most of your questions."

"Why?"

"Because I'm working on being less selfish and immature and more empathetic."

"Do you know what empathy is?"

"I might not have gone to college, *doctor*, but I'm not an ignorant."

"I'm not asking for the definition. I'm asking if you know what it feels like."

"Oh," I was taken aback by her question. "I suppose."

"Give me evidence."

"I…took into account my family's feelings when I decided to come to the hospital."

"Selfless, good. Not enough to be empathetic though. What are you missing?"

"I guess I could be more considerate…and understanding."

"Some people say empathy is a skill you are born with, others believe it can be learnt and honed. I'm somewhere in the middle. I do believe you can learn to be more receptive, open, forgiving, and as you say, considerate and understanding."

"How?"

"Practice. Objective number three, think before you act. Pause for a few instants before you make a choice. Breathe, take into account the consequences, the present, the future, your feelings and the feelings of others."

"I don't think I've ever done that."

"Can you picture a scenario where you are capable of doing it? Close your eyes and let's practice again." And so we did, a few times, until I was content with the outcome. J.M. taught me some relaxation and breathing exercises afterwards, and we talked about my repetitive behavioral patterns. "Why are you so attached to your old behavioral patterns?"

"I guess…it's all I know," I said truthfully.

"How do you think you can learn healthier behaviors?"

"Listening to you?" I sort of joked.

"Responding to your needs in different ways, I'd say. Objective number four, recognize your usual thoughts, and the emotions and behaviors they elicit. You will write them down for a few weeks in three columns, and we will try to find different alternatives to them together, okay?"

"Deal. Is that my assignment?"

"Yes." She stood up and signaled the time. "The empanadas were lovely, by the way," she complimented me as she walked me to the door.

"Thanks," I responded, and a warm feeling invaded me all of a sudden. It wasn't her compliment; I think I had just discovered I wanted to cook for a living.

*   *   *

"I quite enjoy writing, to tell you the truth," I began, in what was my sixth session with Dr. J.M. Carroll. I wasn't using crutches anymore and I only had a slight limp when it was humid. So every day in Ireland, basically. It was March already, and Will's birthday was fast approaching.

"Good, there's a very interesting therapy I'm exploring, it's called Narrative Therapy," J.M explained. "Would you like to choose a moment of your life and write a chapter about it, and then we can discuss it together?"

"Yeah…sounds entertaining. I think I'll start by my second suicide attempt, the one on May last year."

"What do you think writing about your life might bring you?"

"Perspective, for sure."

"Hopefully. And a sense of stability and continuity. I'd like those concepts, along with perseverance, to be your next objective."

"I drop out of things the moment they turn complicated, J.M. I don't have any long standing romantic relationships. I don't even think I have friends."

"I agree it was your pattern of behavior for a long time. But give me an example to prove your statement wrong."

"This therapy?"

She smiled. "Very good. Anything else?"

"My family? But I can't really drop out of them, or them out of me. They are forced to tolerate me."

"Someone you always mention isn't."

"Damn it, J.M.," I kept vomiting stream of curses. "Will Cadillac."

She grinned and nodded. "He can teach you a thing or two about perseverance, huh."

"He makes me feel good, J.M., even better than the meds." I looked outside the window. "But I screwed things up with him, many times."

"And, somehow, he's always still in your life."

"Somehow."

"Why did you ruin your chances with him if he makes you feel good?"

"I don't know."

"Try again."

"He makes me feel *everything*…and when I feel…it's all so intense, I feel too much, so I shut down."

"So back to session one. You push away to avoid the pain. Objective number six, avoid avoiding behavior. Who is an expert on avoidance, sleeping right next to you every night?"

I snickered. "Choi!"

J.M. grinned again. "She's one of the loveliest people I've ever met, on and off the job. I'm not her psychiatrist at the moment, but I talked to her plenty of times on her first admission. I think she'd be open to tell you what she's learnt about avoidance."

"I'll give it a try."

"Will you be polite and nice?"

"I said I'd give it a try!"

"What's the worst that can happen if you are a perfectly decent, good, nice person, and people don't respond in the same way?"

"It'd be painful, I suppose."

"And what's the worst that can happen when you feel pain Lucy?"

"I go to the extremes we always talk about."

"Have you learnt any alternatives during these weeks?"

"Yes."

"Do you think you'd be able to put them in practice?"

"Why else am I here, if not to try out everything you suggest," I said laughing.

"Do you think you have a high tolerance for emotional pain?"

"Shit no, J.M!"

"Do you know anyone who does? Anyone who's been perfectly decent, and good, and nice, and whom you've treated unfairly many times, who has felt pain and been hurt, and still reacted in a way you wouldn't have?"

I slapped my forehead and squinted my eyes in regret. "Will fucking Cadillac."

"So that's your assignment for the week. A chat with Choi about avoidance and a chat with Will about persevering despite the pain."

*　　*　　*

"Whoa, that was a very interesting read, Lucy," J.M. exclaimed. "You definitely have a talent for writing."

"Thanks." I bowed proudly. It was week 10 of our therapy together and I felt like I had never felt before. Like an adult, possibly. I was given time off during the weekends, and I frequently visited Choi's Korean family, who were incredibly loving. Sean, Camille, Marco and Tilly all came to visit, and my mom had bought a ticket for the approximate date of my discharge, in 5 weeks, on Monday April 8th. She would be staying for three months, until after my birthday. She had asked for an extended leave at work due to her daughter's illness.

"What if I had said that it was a crappy read?"

"I would have been highly offended," I admitted, grimacing. "It is my life story, after all."

"Do you think people will always agree, like, or praise what you do? What if someone doesn't enjoy your cooking?"

"How dare them!" I said, pretending to be scandalized.

"Lucy, how would you feel?"

"Down, probably."

"Why?"

"I honestly don't know…" I knew by then what she'd say in response, so I quickly added, "maybe I give too much importance to what unimportant people say, and little important to what the important ones do."

"Grand, I agree. You are so smart, I love it," she cheered. "It makes my job so much easier." We both laughed. "We are fast approaching your release, and I'd like to discuss to final objectives. This is one of them, your seventh, if I'm not mistaken. Build a higher tolerance for frustration."

"How do I do that?" I asked suspiciously.

"You won't achieve it in five weeks, it's a lifelong exercise, but we'll start with a little role playing." We acted several scenarios where she was an annoyed customer who disliked my food, then she was a psychologist who made up some nonsense about my daddy issues and kept calling me Borderline, and finally, she was Will, telling me he had realized I wasn't good enough for him. God, did it hurt!

"I failed all the exercises, didn't I?"

"You failed only if you didn't realize that in all of them you were invaded by anger first, answering very irritated, and only then did you apply the things we learnt together."

"True," I answered, feeling empowered. "Let's try it again." By the end of the series of role playing exercises, I had circles of sweat in my sweatshirt. Lovely.

"Why do you think I chose cooking, your father and Will as the main subjects?"

"They are definitely sensitive topics," I recognized.

"Why?"

"Because I care about them. They are the things I feel passionate about."

"You made your life so far about finding your father, that was the driving force that brought you here. Has it been fruitful?"

"Not in the way I initially envisioned. I expected to find him alive and well in Galway, teaching in a school, with a new family, and hating him for having abandoned me."

"How do you feel about it now?"

"I think...I understand him, J.M." The abrupt conclusion blew me away. Shit. "I think, for once, I see why he did what he did. He was trying to protect his little girl from his sick mind. I don't think it's an excuse, but I have stopped blaming him, and my mom, for not fighting for him."

"Anyone else you have stopped blaming in the process?" She winked at me.

"Yeah, it wasn't my fault either."

"Are you ready to find a new purpose in life then, that's only about your fulfillment?"

I beamed. "Last objective maybe?"

"Exactly," she affirmed. "And its assignment I presume you will like." She reclined her chair and retrieved a book from the shelf behind. "Read Viktor Frankl's book, *Man in Search for Meaning*, and write down, as soon as you finish, your thoughts and feelings it provoked."

"Awesome," I said, taking the book.

"I won't be here next week, since I'm on annual leave. So I'll see you in two weeks, which gives you plenty of time to finish the book. It's a fast, enjoyable read, though deeply moving."

"Great. Are you traveling to Argentina?"

"I wish," she answered, "but I don't have enough time. I'll just chill out with my pets in my house."

"TELL ME ALL ABOUT THEM," I demanded, opening my eyes widely, and she laughed in response.

"Well, where to start...my husband had a Beagle before we met, Leinster, he is 6 now. That's our oldest," she explained, and her eyes sparkled as she spoke. "We then adopted three rescues, we call them 'the half-breeds'. Ringo, Lilac and Sweden. We decided to name them after things we liked, following Leinster's tradition, which is my husband's rugby team." I smiled, and she kept talking. "One day, leaving the hospital, a tiny black kitten without an eye crossed my path. That's my girl, Silver. And finally, we have a mischievous, ginger, puffy cat, who we suspect has a double life. Every time he comes back from his disappearances, he looks chubbier."

"He definitely has another family, J.M. That cheating rascal!"

"I know! So we call him Drizzle, because he's almost always around, but he is an unpredictable pain in the arse."

"Do you have 'human' kids too?" I marked the inverted commas in the air.

She shook her head. "My husband is an engineer, he's really fast in the brain, but his…swimmers a little slow down below." I blushed slightly…oops.

"Oh…I'm sorry. I didn't mean to pry or anything."

"You're grand," she said smiling. "We are starting the second course of treatment in a couple of months. Fingers crossed."

"Well, I hope you enjoy your time off with your furry kids in the meantime, they sound lovely," I responded gently, from a true, kind place of my heart I hadn't ventured into ever before.

*   *   *

"So this is the plan," I began excitedly. "I have enrolled in Dublin Community College for a three-year Bachelor's Degree in Culinary Arts. And…wait for it…drumrolls…I have chosen Creative Writing and Spanish as my electives for the first year, they give me extra credits. The curriculum seems very interesting, and it gives me plenty of time to find a part-time job in a restaurant, which shouldn't be so hard being an Irish citizen and having some experience in cooking."

"That is fabulous," J.M. congratulated me. "When do you start?"

"September."

"Have you thought where you will live?"

"The Social Worker helped my mom find a small two-bedroom apartment close to the city center. She rented it online. After she leaves, ideally, I'd like to cover for its expenses…so I asked Choi if she'd like to be my roommate."

"And...?"

"She moves in in August."

"Brilliant!" J.M. clapped. "Sounds like a solid plan. Remember I'm part of the plan too, for better or worse. We will see each other every month in the outpatient clinic in town. As soon as you are discharged on Monday, you can call and arrange the first appointment." She handed me a card with all the details. "You will also see an individual psychotherapist there every week."

"Okay. I have to keep going to physio twice a week for two more months, until I finish the six-month treatment. So I'll be quite busy."

"How do you feel about living with your mom again, after almost a year?"

I hesitated for a few seconds. "I'm not sure yet. But if I survived the sessions with you, I can survive her intense mothering."

"You both deserve some healthy time together." I nodded in agreement. "I'd like to meet her at her earliest convenience, we can arrange it in a few weeks."

"Sure."

"Who's picking you up on Monday?"

"My grandma, Tilly, I think you met her in one of the family meetings."

"Oh yes, I remembered your description, but she was even more remarkable in person. Quite the character!"

"She's so cool, she even asked my cousin Marco to install Skype in the laptop I left behind at her house. That way, she can continue pestering me with her cooking lessons and telling me off for being too thin."

J.M. laughed. "Typical Irish granny."

"My grandpa has arthrosis in both knees, so he can't travel much. It'll be nice to video chat with him too."

"Did you imagine thinking, feeling, let alone saying that four months ago?"

I shook my head. "I still have a lot of work to do, you know, with myself."

J.M nodded. "You have time, *we* have time. The worst part's over. Is there anything else you'd like to talk about before we finish our last session?"

"Yes." I jumped up and gave her a tight hug. "That was an impulse, sorry, but it was the only way I could find to show you how thankful I am."

She hugged me back. "I'm officially handing you the degree for having passed the 18-week intensive course in Brain Rewiring."

We both laughed. "Mind workout sure does burn some calories."

"And some other nuisances too, I hope." She winked and me and led me to the door one final time.

CHAPTER SEVENTEEN

BURNT TRAVELER

December 2006

"*Traveler:*
If the colors of the skies
could all clash into a tale,
it'd be a life of endless lives,
and a sea worthy to sail.

When the morning hits the dark.
When the winter cuts the spring.
When the silence takes the heart,
new adventures make it sing.

I will travel to the frontiers
of the land that gave us birth,
until I reach the shiniest river
in this planet we call Earth.

Let me find my way to bliss
with a pocket full of nuisance.
I will always choose the abyss

over the shelter of ignorance.

Instead of dreams of plastic dolls,
I saw waves with dancing ships,
writing stories of lost calls
that would one day invite me in.

My secret thoughts playfully juggle
in the midst of air and fire,
intertwined in a love struggle
with the journeys I desire.

I am one with my own world,
even though it has no borders.
It is filled with gems and pearls,
of the woods I dream to wander.

Love me now, for I am free,
but tomorrow I'll be there,
where my spirit finds a tree
full of stories of nowhere."

Scattered claps erupted around the room, the professor was smiling pleasantly at the body of students as she prompted them to be more expressive.

"That was wonderful, Lucy. An amazing glimpse into your dreams," she said, in her thick Easter European accent. "Thank you for sharing." Not that I had a choice. I went back seat, looking down, and refusing to engage in any sort of human contact with my peers.

Strangely enough, Thursdays were my favorite. I had Creative Writing in the morning and Spanish in the afternoon, with a bunch of loud classmates whose Spanish was worse than my Mandarin. There were some Colombians and Mexicans in the group, which the professor didn't find shady at all. Goodness me. After Spanish, I had Baking and Pastry Techniques, my all-time favorite subject. At least from this first semester. The rest of the days were a mixture of Culinary Techniques, Classical Cooking Techniques and a workshop in Public Sanitation and Safety, which might as well could have been an overdose of cyanide. Most of the days, I was home by 6pm, just in time to catch the reruns of *Father Ted*.

Every Friday morning, I had therapy with Mr. O'Callaghan at 9am. Once a month, I also saw my psychiatrist, Dr. J.M. Carroll, one hour before my therapy. My physiotherapy was done, and I had to see the GP once every six months, so I was very well on the path of recovery. Or so I thought.

"Hola menina linda, tudo bem?" that insufferably obnoxious Brazilian guy said to my ear.

"Hola Anthony, todo bien," I responded in Spanish. All good.

"You are very rough," he said in a whisper, intending to be sexy. Ugh, shudders! My creepy radar starting beeping forcefully.

"Tough? Yeah, even more than I look." I started walking away from him as we both exited the College doors, but he trotted behind me and quickly kept up with my fast pace.

"Would you like to join us this Saturday on our Christmas party? 10pm, the *Sugary Latino Club*. I bartend there on the weekends."

"I'd rather jump the Cliffs of Moher at their highest peak, Antonio, than go to a club with you and your pals."

He wiggled a tan finger in my face. "I go by Anthony here." I couldn't believe Choi, my roommate, had a crush on that disgusting character.

"That's a vital piece of information, *Anthony*, which I'm sure my friend Choi will highly appreciate." I resumed my jogging.

"Choi?" He scratched his forehead, pretending not to know who she was. I could murder him right there, in the middle of the street, if it wasn't for the CCTV cameras filming us and all the damn witnesses watching us in a public space.

"Yeah, Choi Ho, my friend, the one you banged one night and then kept flirting with for three months via Messenger. The ones whose hopes you keep getting up to no use."

"Oh, Choi, yeah. Bring her too, sure."

"Go fuck yourself, Anthony," I said, pointing at his face with my Leap Card. I hopped on the bus and gave him the finger, while he broadcasted his repulsive pristine grin to the poor, poor world.

*　*　*

"SAY WE ARE GOING, LUCY, PLEASE!" Choi begged desperately. It was Saturday evening and I was deep into my Sanitation notes.

"My mid-terms start next week Choi, now bugger off."

"OMG Lucy, please, I have no one to go with! All of my friends from med school have their noses in our books."

I raised an eyebrow at her. "Shouldn't you be doing the same, South Korean prodigy?"

"Tomorrow, I promise…but pretty please, come with me today." She knelt on her knees and continued begging. It was a sad sight. "I will cook for a month."

I put my index finger up, really close to her small nose. "Cooking is my forte, lady Ho." She nodded expectantly. "You will do the laundry for a month instead."

"Woo hoo!" she cheered, jumping up and down the room.

"And promise me you won't let Anthony see you so desperate," I threatened her. "It's enough he sees you drooling over his tanned muscles every time you bump into each other."

"Pinky promise!" Choi was still skipping on one foot around our small living room, exultant in her young, hormonal stupidity.

My Skype started ringing. It was Tilly.

"Hi grandma!" I waved at her, spotting Aidan a little behind her, sitting in his rocking chair, as usual. "Hi grandpa!" They both greeted me back.

"Ready for yer cooking lesson? I have prepared a few recipes for ye to go over." She put her huge glasses on.

"Oh, grandma, I'm so sorry, can we do it tomorrow instead?" Her mouth was a thin line of disapproval, and she was goggling at me from above her glasses. "My friend Choi had a...sort of...emergency, let's put it that way."

"Teenagers," she puffed.

"We are 22, grandma."

"Jaysus, even worse. Talk to you tomorrow then, Lucy." She squinted her eyes trying to find the red button.

"Wait grandma! I have a couple of questions on desserts, and I'm sure you can help me. You are the grand expert after all."

"No need to sugar coat it, love. Shoot."

"So remember how I started working in a restaurant a couple of months ago?" She nodded. "I make a killer lemon pie, and my apple tart is to die for. But some customers have complained that my crème brûlée tastes a little burnt, and my chocolate lava cakes aren't volcano-ish enough."

"Well, ye were always keen on the fire, Lucy," she said, sighing. "What do you use to caramelize the crème brûlée?"

"A chef's torch."

"Ah, modern technology, eh." She shook her head. "Use an old-fashioned lighter, and make sure you use caster sugar on top of the custard, not that cheap substitutes I'm sure they make you use." I nodded, jotting down her tips. "And the best way to make a decent lava cake is using frozen chocolate. Listen to me child, chop the dark chocolate evenly, a GOOD one, not a supermarket disgrace, and put it in the freezer as soon as you leave the restaurant. You can use it the following day to fill in the cakes. 12 minutes, 200° oven. Not a minute or a grade more."

I scribbled it all down. "You are the best grandma." She nodded. "Guess what? I got an A in Creative Writing last week."

"Good woman!"

"She takes after her father!" grandpa screamed from behind, unnecessarily loudly.

"SHE CAN HEAR YOU JUST FINE WITHOUT YE YELLING, DEAF PILE OF RUBBISH. And she is a cook, she takes after her grandma!"

"But she is brilliant, so she takes after me!" my grandpa countered, and I thought I saw him stick his tongue out to my grandma's back. I sniggered.

"I take after the three of you, grand, figures I'm so insane." We all laughed. "Now, show me the three babies before I go." Charlie was already stomping on the keyboard before I had finished talking.

*   *   *

"Now, go to the bar and say something you won't regret." I pointed at where Anthony was pouring drinks to a group of swooning ladies, dancing at the beat of the Latin music.

"Like what?" Choi was blushing desperately, her previously neat bun a mess of dark, uneven hairs. It was a little after midnight, and I would have given my good leg to get the heck out of that nightmare.

"Something like...*hey jerk, I have feelings for you. Care to man up and do something about it?*"

She opened her eyes in awe and sheer dread, so I gave her a small push towards the bar, and escaped to the bathroom.

"Excuse me," a deep voice said. "I think you lost this."

"Shite." A cute, blonde guy handed me my bandana. It was the only thing which kept my curls under control in that dampness, and it wasn't like I was going to find a boyfriend in that wretched place. "Thanks."

I started scampering off towards the bathroom, but the guy followed. "Aren't you the girl who read the poem last week?" DAMNED PITS OF HELL. "I think we are on the same Creative Writing class." Not that I would notice, I hadn't spoken to a single soul there, not even during the group projects. "I'm Declan, and you are Lucy, right?"

"Indeed." I shook his hand. "Scottish?"

"As it gets. Glaswegian."

"Good for you," I said, looking at my watch. Damn it, it was only 12.15. "Wow, it's getting really late and I have mid-terms coming up. Nice meeting you Dylan."

"Declan," he corrected me, laughing, and held my arm. I threw him a lethal look. "Let me buy you a drink." He had a very disgusting orange cocktail in his hand.

"I don't drink." He looked surprised. "I did, a lot…that's why. I'm in recovery, sort of." I shrugged. "Not that I'm in rehab, like, *Hi, my name is Lucy and I'm an alcoholic,* kind of thing!"

He put both his hands up, spilling part of his drink on his shirt. "Not judging, Lucy. Would you like to catch a movie instead?"

"What?" He had caught me off guard, completely. "No. I don't know. Maybe. Ask me again in a few months."

"Bye Lucy, Merry Christmas," he said, saluting me, and I rushed out of the club into a taxi. Choi was busy making out with the bartender anyway.

I arrived at our flat on Dame Street, completely unaware that, in the near future, I would mishandle my story with Declan, like I always did, since he would fall for me harder that I had fallen over the cliff, except that all I could offer, was a deep bottom of sharp, rocky edges.

CHAPTER EIGHTEEN

THE ISLE OF SKYE

August 2007

"Declan, please, we've been over this a gazillion times. It's frankly exhausting." I looked up into his light blue eyes. His blonde hair had grown a little longer during the summer, and he had a shadow of a beard. He had a sweet face, which matched his personality like two pieces of a puzzle. "I absolutely hate pictures!"

"But why Lucy? You have the most beautiful eyes," he protested. Ever since he had taken that elective in Photography, he had become intolerable with his damn camera. I couldn't tell him that I despised pictures because my dad loved to take snaps of me with his antique Polaroid when I was a little girl. Declan didn't even know a tenth of my story.

"I just don't, and that's that. Now let me enjoy the landscape."

We were heading towards the Isle of Skye in a ferry from the Highlands. Declan's grandparents ran an Inn in the Scottish Island, and he had invited me to spend a weekend over. We had first toured around Glasgow for a day, but I had refused to stay overnight, since I didn't want to meet his parents. Not yet, at least. We had been dating casually since April, I had made it abundantly clear I wasn't interested in any sort of exclusive commitment, and he seemed, key word being *seemed*, to understand it.

"Are you on your period? Is that why you are so grumpy?"

"For the love of god, Declan! Who the hell says that?!"

He shrugged, evidently hurt. "I think I'd better go inside."

"Yeah, I think you'd better." Declan scurried inside the ferry, and I stayed outside, enjoying the spectacular panorama and the fresh wind batting my curls.

Declan was textbook perfect in endless ways. He was a responsible Economics student, originally from Glasgow, but who had moved to Dublin because he didn't like the program in the University of Glasgow. His mother's family was Irish, so he was living with his cousins while he studied. His family was apparently quite functional, they were supportive and understanding, from what he described. He had a younger sister, still in High School, an older brother working in Brussels, and plenty of friends from his rugby team. He was caring, hard-working and respectful…and thus bored me immensely.

I didn't particularly dislike spending time with him, he was a perfectly nice guy. But that was the problem, the *perfect* in perfectly. I always felt like a screw-up around him, even if he didn't intend to make me feel that way. After all, he barely even knew I went to therapy. But he lacked that spark, that…mountain of flaws that would make me want to bond with his secret, dark, insane alien. He had no secrets, he was open, confident and sociable, and loved to drag me to his friends' pool parties and rugby matches. I hated pools almost as much as I hated sports. But he didn't bother to ask, because around him, I put the mask on, and pretended to be like any other girl.

When we arrived to the isle, his grandparents were already waiting for us at the docks in their car. He introduced me as his girlfriend. Enough said, this would be a weekend to forget.

*   *   *

Skye was a gorgeous mass of land, interrupted by seaside hills and stone formations. Declan had figured it would be romantic to invite me to the Isle that had given birth to my surname. But the Isle was much more than that, with its uneven terrain, its constantly blowing breeze, and the desolated patches of messy landscape. I felt like it was nature's representation of my soul.

"So, this is our room," Declan announced coyly. *Our*, shit. We had been dating for a few months, but we hadn't reached the *intimacy* arena yet.

"The bed looks cozy." I tossed my backpack over the desk and made my way to the bathroom. But the guy had other plans. He started kissing me passionately, holding me tightly from my waist, and busying one of his hands a little below.

"Okay, pause," I said, catching my breath. He looked confused.

"I thought all was going well." Clueless, as usual.

I nodded. "Yeah, you are great Declan, but…"

"…but?" I sat on the bed and started playing with my curls.

"I haven't been with anyone…"

"Oh," he clapped his forehead and lowered his voice to a mere whisper. "You are a…*virgin?*"

That did it, I couldn't contain the laughter. "Oh no pal…you got it so wrong…that train's been long gone for a good number of years!"

He didn't budge. "What's the problem, then?" He sat next to me, evidently impatient.

"I haven't been with anyone since my last 'relationship', if you could call it like that."

"And you're still hung up on this guy? Is that why you won't let me get closer to you?"

I shook my head. "He's married now, Declan. It's all over between us."

"That doesn't mean your heart knows it's over, Lucy." Ugh, why did he have to be so corny all the time?

"Kiss me, I'll prove it to you." Anything to make him stop talking. And so I got closer to him, as close as he wanted, even if my mind, and definitely my heart, were thousands of miles away.

* * *

"Are we still up for Electric Picnic next weekend?"

I nodded, relieved the taxi was about to drop me off at my flat. It was Sunday at 8pm, and I had a Food Technology class early the following morning. Choi was a good friend; she would understand I wasn't in the mood for sharing. Besides, she had barely overcome her latest episode of depression, following that damned Brazilian player's mischiefs. Anthony had broken her heart so many times, that one day it had failed to find the way to mend itself alone, and she had to get a psychiatric helping hand. I would have murdered that piece of shit if it hadn't been for his visa expiring and him going back to Brazil, thank the Immigration Bureau.

"See you there," I said distractedly, and kissed Declan lightly on the cheek.

I entered the flat and jumped into the shower in complete silence, but had to soon exit it like a manic, after hearing Choi's screams.

"OMG Lucy, hurry up! You are NOT going to like this!"

Damn it. I put on my underwear, robe and slippers and hurried to the living room. Choi was looking particularly flustered, and turned her laptop around to show me the screen. Clueless, arsehole, stupid Declan not only had taken pictures of our whole trip, but had uploaded them to Facebook, whatever ass webpage that was.

"Choi, make me an account." She goggled at me, terrified. "NOW!"

Once the account was made and he had accepted my "friend request", all courtesy of Choi's aid, I started commenting on all the pictures.

"Sorry, that's not Lucy Skye, like Declan McAdams claims. That's a product of his imagination."

"Look at that face, it almost looks like that poor girl completely hates being photographed."

"Oh, and look at that frown, that girl definitely despises that pathetic excuse for a gentleman."

A chat window popped open on the corner of the screen, and Choi disappeared to the kitchen to make tea.

"What do you think you're doing?" Declan typed.

"Trying to ruin your life, like you ruined mine."

"Don't be so dramatic, Lucy. It's nothing big. I just wanted to share all the good things that are happening to us."

"Try sharing with me first, ok?"

"I'm sorry. I'll delete them if you want."

"Of course you will delete them! My family could all have Facebook by now for all I know, and they will see those pics and start asking questions."

"So you are embarrassed to be seen with me? Is that it? They can't see my photos if we are not friends anyway."

"I couldn't care less! And you are delusional, man. Good luck with your nice life."

"Lucy, wait…don't leave like this. Would you like to talk on the phone?"

"I'd rather talk to Stalin's zombie body, thank you very much. See you on Saturday."

"OK. I love you…"

What on the Earth's wretched core had he said? He *loved* me? By chat? I disconnected that whole circus before I grabbed one of my cooking knives and slit his throat.

*   *   *

"Did I tell you I hate festivals?" I asked Choi, for the millionth time.

"Maybe six or seven times already," she screamed over the music. Some dumb band was blasting through the amplifiers, and pretty girls in white dresses with headbands made of flowers and cowboy boots, moved flirtingly to the tune. Pretty boys in skinny pants and shiny sunglasses checked them out, all a sad symbol of human mating.

"We're back, girls!" said Declan, accompanied by his Canadian friend Reed. They had brought refreshments for us and Choi's baby brother, Park. He had just turned 18, and his parents figured going to the Electric Picnic with his 23-year-old sister would be a most suitable present. Bless his soul.

Choi blushed very conspicuously every time Reed tried to engage her in conversation, but I was too focused on hating on Declan to mind her. He held my hand and dragged me behind a tent.

"Hey stranger, you have been avoiding me all week." He tried to kiss me, but I shoved him back.

"My psychiatrist, and Choi, taught me avoidance is never a good resort," I explained, and he grimaced at the mention of the word 'psychiatrist'. "Look, Declan, this isn't going anywhere."

"What do you mean?"

"I mean that you," I pointed at his chest, "and me," I pointed at mine, "isn't going to work."

"But...did you read what I told you the other day on Facebook chat?"

"Yeah, and I'm...flattered." He jolted in surprise. "I really, really care about you."

"But you are in love with someone else, is that it?" Sure, have it your way.

"I hadn't noticed I had these strong feelings until I met him in person," I said, playing along his delusion, trying very hard to refrain from laughing.

"Who the hell is he? I'm going to kill him!"

"No, Declan, come on...you are better than that."

Choi, Park and Reed came looking for us and found us arguing behind the tent.

"Bad time?" asked Reed. Declan nodded and I shook my head in unison.

"Lucy was just telling me she's in love with someone else," Declan blurted out furiously.

"Oh, yeah, Will..." said Choi, like the idiot friend she was. I stared at her murderously. "I mean...*will* they ever find the way to be together?" She turned deep scarlet and I wanted nothing more than to slap her.

"Maybe we will." I pulled Park's shirt towards me and kissed him on the mouth. I thought he would pass out. Choi started laughing and Reed was gaping at us, slightly disgusted, but I didn't have time to react, Declan was already punching him repeatedly on the face.

"OH JAYSUS!" I screamed, Park had fallen flat to the muddy ground. Park was a slender teenager, and Declan had the arm of a seasoned rugby player. "GET THE HELL OUT OF HERE DECLAN, GET THE HELL OUT OF MY LIFE!" Anger management issues, then that was perfect boy's secret, dark alien. Even the most immaculate of angels have one.

Thank god, the emergency doctor said Park only had a broken nose, and as Choi's parents put him in the car, he mouthed at me "Best. Birthday. Ever."

CHAPTER NINETEEN

MOCHA SHAKE

December 2008

"Are you really leaving? Have you thought it through? DON'T DO THIS TO ME, CHOI!" I was clinging to her shirt.

"Lucy, come on, I've talked about it with my mom, my therapist, my psychiatrist, and you maybe...five hundred times?" she said, snatching her sleeve from me. "It's you I'm worried about."

"I'll be grand...you are the one moving in with a guy!" Her engagement ring sparkled under our living room lights. My living room lights, I shall say.

"Are you sure this isn't about you, and not me?"

I pretended to be scandalized. "How dare you, Ho? When have I ever made things about me?"

"Twice a day, on a good day." We both laughed. "I think you might be projecting your own fears of never finding love on me."

"Ah, come on Choi, don't give me that crappy psychobabble. I'm genuinely concerned for your welfare." She rolled her eyes and kept closing her bags.

"Reed will be here any time now. Promise to behave?"

"Cross my heart," I lied, helping her with the bag. "What did you mean when you said I was afraid?"

"See? There, you just did it. We are talking about you now," she answered, laughing. I threw her a jacket. "When was the last time you spoke to Will?"

"What? I don't know, we speak almost every day. Why?"

"That's precisely why, you speak to him, but do you really talk? Does he know how you feel, for instance?"

"Shut up, Dr. Ho. I don't feel anything, I'm an…empty rubbish bag."

"Riiiiight, that's why you mention him 15 times a day. On a good day." I threw her a pair of gloves. "You are head over heels for the guy."

"Speaking of guys, I think someone knocked." Thank you Reed, saved by the knock.

Okay, so maybe my concern was a little about me. Reed entered the living room and smiled at Choi, who kissed him for what felt like half an hour. A feeling similar to unease tightened my chest. Would I ever find what they had? I'd had the chance with Will, and spoiled it, of course. He was happily married to insipid Sarah now. Maybe I was destined to be forever alone. Or become a nun.

"When are the results for your Canadian exams arriving?" I asked Choi, crossing my arms.

"January."

"Do you have your applications ready?"

"Yes." Reed stifled a laugh.

"Will you promise to visit?"

"Lucy, I'm moving in with Reed in Phibsborough, it's a 15-minute walk from here, if you walk REALLY slowly."

"But Choi, it's the…" I dropped my voice into a shady whisper, "…*north side.*"

Now they both chuckled openly. "I promise I'll take care of myself."

"And will you promise to text me?"

"Yes."

"Call me every day?"

"Yes."

"Eat well? You are losing weight with all the stress from the wedding and the exams."

"You are worse than her mother, Lucy," Reed said, still laughing.

"And that's saying a lot," Choi responded, rolling her eyes again. Oh my god, I was 50-year-old usurping the body of a young woman.

"Fine, go you two. Happy days." I gave Choi a hug and waved at Reed. They grabbed the bags and left me alone with my Classical Cuisine textbook.

I had been working for two and a half years as an assistant in a restaurant down south. My job was part time, I only had three fixed days, of four hours each. I was mainly in charge of the dessert area, and it gave me plenty of time to study and go to therapy. But my last semester in College would be a lot lighter than the previous ones, having only practical courses, so I spoke to the manager, who offered me to work from Monday to Saturday, from 2pm to 8pm. That also entailed a leap in responsibilities, and thankfully, in the paycheck as well. I would be home a lot less and would be able to save more than 200 euros a month, but I still needed to find a roommate as soon as possible.

A soft knocking on the door interrupted my musings. I assumed it was Choi, having forgotten some of her belongings. It was a woman, but not my former roommate and friend.

"Are you going to give your mom a hug or what?" Olivia asked, and I jumped in her arms.

"Mom! What are you doing here?" I hugged her again and led her to my tiny living room couch, where she placed her bag. She had traveled seven hours on a plane, but she still seemed like she had been taken from a catalog. I probably looked like a heap of dirt next to her, wearing leggings, a sweatshirt and a make-up free, freckled face.

"I thought I'd surprise you for the holidays! Don't worry, I'm only staying for two weeks," she added hastily.

"God, I missed you so much! We haven't seen each other in over two years!"

"And whose fault is that?"

I tossed her a cushion. "Shut up. I'll go put the kettle on."

"Oh, darling, before I forget, I have to give you something," she said, opening her bag. She had adopted that mysterious tone she liked so much, only to spike my interest. "Will sent you a Christmas present."

Jesus Christ and the twelve Apostles! My heart fell to the underground basement. Olivia handed me a large envelope, which, naturally, held a drawing inside. It was an oil painting of a single, impressive violet, floating on the background of a sky of diamonds. I gulped at the beauty of the gift, and told my mom I would leave just for a little while to get it framed, before the shops closed. Lies, of course. I went straight into the tattoo parlor a few meters from the flat, where I inked forever behind my earlobe a tiny replica of the painting. I vowed that very instant that I would never show it to anyone but Will, because he was, and always would be my number 10. He had changed, and incurably saved, my entire life.

* * *

The black girl at the door was *big*. She was indeed big in more than one sense of the word. She had big, frizzy hair, big silver hoop earrings, big eyelashes, big, glossy lips, a big physique, and an even bigger attitude.

"Hello, you Lucy?"

"Yeah," I said, inspecting her animal print tights. "And you are?"

"Monike Charice Jewel Lawless, pleasure to meet you." She had very big fingernails too. "You can call me Mocha Jelaw, pronounced like 'jellow'."

"Right, hello. You can call me Lucy, pronounced just like that. So I take it you saw my ad for a new roommate?"

"Hm-hhh," she said, barging in and making herself comfortable on the couch. "I'm an ideal candidate, I'm not so sure about a pale girl who can't hold her steak." She eyed me from head to toe with disgust. I suddenly felt very self-conscious. At least she wouldn't eat me if ended up secluded in a zombie apocalypse.

"I'm quite ideal, too, Miss Jelaw." God, what a stupid name. "Where are you from?"

"Queens, New York. You local?"

"Something like that, I'm originally from Cleveland."

She ignored my answer. "So, I will take the room. I'm a make-up and hair stylist, so I might make noises with the hair dryer when I'm practicing my dos. I always like to eat alone in my room watching TV, I'll get one installed tomorrow. I shower every night and don't like being bothered after 8pm."

"Sounds brilliant," I said truthfully. I'd be home after 8 every almost every day anyway. "When can you move in?"

"Give me a skinny hand, gurl. My bags are downstairs."

*　*　*

It was Friday May 1st 2009 and I was about to hand my final exam on Culinary Management. Sweat trickled down my forehead as I signed the paper and gave it to the professor, who winked at me in confidence. At least one of us had faith in me. I was in the hallway, cluttered with students, when I heard the guard call my name.

"Lucila Skye? Is there a Lucila Skye here?" a male garda bellowed above the racket of the students. I raised my hand, my heart beating in my mouth. Every single soul turned to look at me. The guard signaled me to follow him to the car, where a female garda was waiting.

"What's this about?" I asked timidly, barely finding the strength to speak.

"We will talk when we reach the station," the guard answered, and he closed the door to the patrol car.

I had never been inside a police station in my whole life. All the crimes I had committed started parading before my eyes, and I wondered which one of them had got me arrested. Irresponsible drinking at 15? Defiance of authority? Having an 18-year-old innocent boy get punched by an older guy? Oh my god, my vision went blurry.

"Come inside, please, Miss Skye." The male garda ushered me into an interrogation room, where two more gardaí were waiting inside, one of them the policewoman from the car. I was trembling from red curls to toes.

"May I ask what happened?"

"We will ask the questions first," the female garda said in an unpleasant voice. Okay, so she was playing bad cop. Remember CSI Lucy, come on. "Could you please tell us what you did today Miss Skye?"

Shit, I was in deep shit trouble, and I couldn't remember what I had done wrong. "Fridays are my busiest days," I answered, in a thin copy of my normal voice. "I woke up at 7am, took a shower, had a small breakfast and headed to the Psychiatric Outpatient Clinic in Parnell Square. I had an appointment with my psychiatrist, Dr. J.M. Carroll at 8am, and then therapy with my psychologist, Mr. O'Callaghan, at 9. We finished around 10."

"May we ask why it is that you are seeing them?" the female guard continued.

I wasn't sure if they were entitled to ask such things, but never mind. Better play along. "I have a personality disorder. I've been in treatment for a couple of years."

"So nuttin' serious like being Schizo or sum' like that?" the male guard asked gently. The woman shot him a sideways glance.

"Well, severity depends on how you live your illness, I guess." He looked at me in complete befuddlement. "I mean, it's subjective…but no, nothing terrible." He jotted something down.

"What did you do then?" the policewoman proceeded.

"I took the bus on O'Connell street to my School, I had a final exam at 10.45. I'm about to graduate as a Bachelor in Culinary Arts. had just finished the exam when you came looking for me."

The man nodded. "Grand, yeah."

"Do I need an attorney, sorry, solicitor or something?" Small droplets of sweat were tickling the sides of my face. The male guard chuckled.

"Nah love, you are not a suspect in my book," he said lightly. "You couldn't hurt a fly!" He laughed again, holding his large belly. "Stay put with my mate Connor here." He placed a hand on the third officer's shoulder, who hadn't spoken a word, and looked young and bored. "We will have to check your story. Be back in a jiffy." Both older gardaí exited the room, and I could feel sweat pads forming in my shirt.

"Do you mind if I have a glass of water?" I croaked to the younger guard.

"Suit yourself." I stood up and welcome the cold taste of the water from the dispenser. "Do I have the right to make a call?"

The young policeman laughed. "You are not under arrest; you can call whomever you want." He showed me to a payphone just outside the room. I retrieved my mobile and dialed Bruno's office. It'd be around 8am in Cleveland.

"Cruz, Hawkins and Mitchell, who am I speaking with?" the receptionist greeted me with a chirpy voice.

"Hi, this is Lucy Skye," I said in a shaky voice. "I need to speak to my uncle...erm, Mr. Bruno Cruz. Please tell him it's urgent." The receptionist transferred me to his intern, all the while listening to *Für Elise*. After what felt like a hellish eternity, Bruno picked up.

"Lucy, are you alright? What happened?"

"Bruno, oh my god, I'm at a police station!"

"Lucy, what did you do?"

"Nothing, I swear! I don't even know why I'm here!"

"Okay, calm down. Is there anyone there with you?"

"No."

"You have the right to refuse answering their questions until a lawyer arrives. I'll hop on a plane as soon as I can."

"No, no uncle Bruno...you don't have to do that. Oh wait, they are coming back. They said they would check my story. I'm so scared, please don't tell mom."

"It's going to be okay darling, keep calm. They can't hold you if they have no evidence against you."

"Thank you uncle, I'll call you tonight. Love you."

"Love you too darling."

The male guard placed his large hand on my shoulder and led me into the room again. "So, Miss Skye. Your story checked. Both doctors confirmed you attended their respective appointments, and there's CCTV footage of you taking the buses at 7.31am to the clinic and 10.12am to the university. You are free to go."

"Just before you leave, do mind leaving us a sample of your handwriting?" the woman guard asked, a little more gently than before.

"What? Yes! No! Wait! What happened?"

"The restaurant where you work has been set on fire. CCTV footage shows a woman entering the premises at 8.26am, and leaving promptly after. There was an explosion a few minutes after that," the male officer explained.

"Oh my god! Is everyone okay?"

"An old lady who lived in the contiguous apartment block suffered extensive injuries and sadly passed away."

"WHAT? Oh Jaysus, I can't believe it." I covered my mouth and started crying. The young officer handed me a box of tissues. "What do you need my handwriting for?"

"We found a note that said '*I, Lucy, did this because I'm crazy and hate the world*' stuck on the front door of the contiguous building. The manager of the restaurant gave us a list of the employees and your named popped up," the woman explained. "We'd like to compare it with your handwriting." I retrieved my notes for the exam from my bag and handed them to her.

"Good, we are all set." The policeman clapped his hands and smiled at me.

"We'll give you a call if we need further assistance from your part," the woman added, and I nodded, still shaking all over.

"Enjoy your weekend," the young guard said, waving lazily at me, and that I would do. The word *'enjoy'* had just reached new and unknown levels of importance. I seized my phone and called Will.

*　　*　　*

It was Monday May 11th when Sharkeisha Kelly Jennifer Lawless, Mocha's sister, opened the door after the first knock. Shake Jelaw, as she preferred to be called, had traveled to Ireland to see her older sister's big participation in a fashion show that week. Mocha Shake sibling love, sisterhood…a deep bond I would never even begin to fathom.

"Lucy, I think it's for you. This white meat sure ain't my siste's."

"Hayell to the no!" Mocha yelled at the sight of Will. Oh my god, it was Will! "This must be the guy she gushes about every damn day."

"That skinny piece o' ass?" Shake asked incredulously, assessing Will's bum. He blushed lightly.

"We'd better get goin'." Mocha grabbed her handbag and her "little" sister, and slammed the door behind them.

I ran into Will's arms. "What the hell do you think you are doing here, Cadillac?!?"

"So you almost got arrested and you think I would miss how your story continues? Not a chance in the world." He was still holding me tightly, like he would never let me go, and time got suspended for the tiniest instant. But he had brought a small satchel, so he wouldn't be staying long.

"I haven't seen you in an eternity." He felt warm and sweet and imperfect as always.

"I know. I missed your curls," he whispered, and I had to let go of his arms to stop myself doing something completely wrong. Probably not illegal, but definitely immoral.

"I missed all of you," I whispered back, and looked away. "You'll be relieved to know they found the person responsible for the fire…a detective called earlier today and said the main suspect is one of the owners. I have to go to the station tomorrow to give them all the information I can, but I barely knew her."

"Crazy world, huh," he responded in a dulled voice that wasn't due to exhaustion, I knew him all too well. Something felt...off.

"Yeah, well, they think she did it for the insurance money, and tried to pin it on me given my 'psychiatric' status."

"Bitch." He squeezed my hand. "I'm glad that nightmare's over."

"Tell me about it." I put the kettle on, and Will sat at the table. "The way they treat 'us' makes me even madder. People with psychiatric illnesses, I mean. Nobody would dare judge or try to frame a diabetic because he takes medication or sees his doctor, would they? But *I* am thinking of not saying I take psych tablets in my next job interview, *I* get judgmental looks when people see my scars, and *I* got stuck in a mess with the police, all because I am a 'weirdo'. How fair is that?"

"People fear what they don't understand, and they think that because we see a psychiatrist or behave 'differently', we are insane. And being insane means being dangerous." I flipped a knife crazily in the air as I chopped chocolate chips to make cookies. "Do you have plans after you graduate?"

"Well, my last final is this Friday. There's a party in some hotel that evening, but I have an interview early on Saturday. Besides, I can't stand my classmates. They would be okay if they didn't speak or move or breathe." I mixed the ingredients in the bowl until I was satisfied with the cookie dough.

"So you're not going back to Cleveland yet?"

"No, I don't think so." I put the cookies in the oven.

"Good," he muttered. I turned around to face him.

"Geez, thank you Cadillac!"

"No, I didn't mean it like that." Will took a deep breath. His skin had a greenish tinge, like he was about to be sick. He had dark circles under his eyes, which looked dim and tired. "I think it might be better if you stayed in Ireland for a while."

"So how long are you staying here?"

"I wish I could stay forever, but I fly back on Thursday."

I sighed, taking his hand. "Will, does Sarah know you're here?"

"Nah," he answered, shrugging. More than physically exhausted, he appeared to be emotionally worn out. "I told her I was going to a conference in the UK for a few days. She gave me a whole speech about spending our savings unnecessarily, but well…it was important I came."

"So…why are you really here?" I asked, doing a poor job at hiding my nerves.

"I needed to see you…one last time." To think that for the briefest moment, my heart had dreamt he had come to stay with me forever.

His eyes gave nothing away, no clues, no hints, just pain. "OH MY GOD WILL, ARE YOU DYING?" I started crying desperately, like the drama queen I usually was.

"What? Lucy! No! It's just…" He slouched on the couch and started sobbing, hiding his lovely face in his hands. "You'll never speak to me again."

"Will, what is it?" I crouched so I could level with his eyes, and pressed my forehead against his. "You can tell me anything." He was still sobbing softly, not daring to look up. It took him a good number of minutes to talk again, my heart beating frantically in the meantime, almost as fast as my brain concocted the weirdest theories.

"Sarah is five months' pregnant." Okay, definitely not that theory. "We didn't plan it…but well, we're keeping the baby. It's a girl."

And with those words, my whole world crumbled, like those cookies which spend too much time dipped inside a hot tea. Dreams, love, companionship, hope and everything good that Will was to me, would be forever crushed, forever lost, forever dead.

CHAPTER TWENTY

CITIZEN OF MY WORLD

November 2009

Katakolon, Greece

"*Dear Greek Willympics, this postcard looks very nice on the outside, but it's still raging inside. How dare Sarah hide for four months that she was pregnant? Anyway, how's the baby? I know she's only two months, but has she said my name already? Gosh, I wish I was there with you, and her. The baby, not freaking Sarah. Did you get my latest e-mail? I'll be doing tours of three month cruises around Europe this year. I'll send postcards from the main ports. Insincerely, Lucy in the Skye. P.S: Greece is everything you see in Google and more. I'll e-mail you the pics. November 24th, 2009.*"

Kusadasi, Turkey

"*Dear Willystanbul, I've learnt three things from working in a large cruise's kitchen. One, never trust the waiters. They are minions sent by the devil to Earth to drive the cooks crazy. Two, don't drink water from the tap. I want to vomit just by thinking of my last stomach flu. Three, you need lots of books for your spare time. I think I've learnt The Raven by Poe by heart. Turkey is stunning, just like Greece, the perfect balance between ancient ruins and colorful beaches. I'm glad the baby is okay; she looks like*" *an angel. Wish you were here. Insincerely, Lucy in the Skye. P.S: Just in case I don't manage to get a connection for the holidays, Merry Christmas and Happy New Year. Not to Sarah. Ugly wishes to her :p December 20ᵗʰ, 2009."*

Civitavecchia, Italy

"Dear Willysseum of Rome, this might sound odd, but I'm actually glad this is the last port. I had the time of my life, but goodness me, how I need a holiday. They are paying me grossly, so I'll be able to save some money, if I don't spend it all on traveling. Italians are some much like Argentineans that it makes me want to laugh. And the cheek of you, remember when you almost went to Argentina for your honeymoon and I freaked out? I'll be the one to take you there, some day. Wish you were here, I miss all of you. Talk to you when I get back from my holidays. Insincerely, Lucy in the Sky. January 16ᵗʰ, 2010."

Lisbon, Portugal

"Dear Willsbon, Portugal reminds me of that creep Anthony, the one that tortured poor Choi. 'They speak the tongue of the devil', she used to say. I miss her. She's married now and doing her specialty in Family Medicine in Toronto. Who would have thought I would ever have a female friend? She should have gone for Psychiatry and save us all some money. We could start a whacko club, our kids would be so proud someday! I remember today is Valentine's Day, so Happy Day…best friend? Or something. Anyway. Bye. Insincerely, Lucy in the Skye. P.S: Did that sound romantic? I didn't mean to. Since we are on the subject, try not to get too romantic tonight and knock Sarah up again, okay? There, that sounded more like me. February 14ᵗʰ, 2010."

Agadir, Morocco

"Dear Willy, which rhymes with chili, the only thing I've tasted since we arrived here, how are things? Your e-mails depress me a little, except when you send me pictures of your beautiful baby girl. Is because you just turned the old age of 27? It's sweltering hot in Morocco, and my curls look like fusilli in a tomato sauce. Tempting, huh. I'll finish this tour in France

and then I'm off to the Baltic in the summer. Wish you were here, having chili sweats with me. Insincerely, Lucy in the Skye. P.S: you know I'll complain of the cold once I'm up north, right? March 21ˢᵗ, 2010."

Marseille, France

"Dear Willfel Tower, total cliché, but bear with me. If I don't get off this cruise in the next few days, I will murder crew, passengers, and food alike. Can you murder food? I don't know. See? I'm rambling. I can barely see straight enough to write. Damn cruise and damn cooking and ideas that get into my head and then I regret them. At least I'm making good money, and I'll be off to Paris next week. Can't wait to send you the pictures of Eurodisney, I bet all of my savings that you'll have a panic attack just by looking at the rides. Last night I dreamt you were singing La Marsellaise in the Bastille, holding a French flag. Stop messing with my head. Still, I wish you were here, stealing my popcorns while we watch a cheesy movie. Insincerely, Lucy in the Skye. April 21ˢᵗ, 2010."

Riga, Latvia

"Dear Willinter, that was so lame. I couldn't find a pun with Latvia, and it's not even winter. My apologies. The scenery is spectacular, I had never been so far up north in my life, and I think I'm in love! How is my platonic godchild? I know Sarah would never make me godmother, but let me dream at least. A fellow cook lent me Wuthering Heights, you would definitely love it. Think of me when you read it. Insincerely, Lucy in the Skye. May 17ᵗʰ 2010."

Stockholm, Sweden

"Dear Willckoholm Syndrome, J.M. had described the beauty of Sweden, but her words fell short. It's truly mesmerizing. Stockholm is indeed the 'Venice of the North', and the people are just too beautiful to be true. Damn their good genes. The shortest one is three heads taller than I am, and the darkest hair I've seen is the color of a banana. You have a soft spot for blonds as I recall, you'd better not come here. Now I'm in a bad mood, see what you do? Insincerely, Lucy in the Skye. P.S: I'm mad

at you, but e-mail me your thoughts on Wuthering Heights anyway. June 8th 2010."

Edinburgh, Scotland

"Dear William Wallace, we finally made port in the UK. Edinburgh is definitely top five of my favorite cities in the world. Or maybe top ten, there are so many! I'd like to see them all again with you, and maybe go to others I haven't been. Not romantically or anything haha! We'd be... travel buddies, as the innocent friends we are. Right, well. I'll be back in Dublin until mid-July, and then I'm flying to Australia. My boss offered me to do six more months of cruises around Asia and Oceania, and who am I to turn it down? I'll call you tomorrow from Dublin. Insincerely, Lucy in the Skye. P.S: I almost called Ireland 'home', but home is where the heart is, and we all know where mine lies. July 1st, 2010."

He picked up after the second tone. It was 9pm in Sydney, and I'd be departing on the cruise the following morning, July 18th 2010.

"Hello?"

"Guess whose birthday it is today? Hint: it's a darling, rather perfect ginger, born on July 17th 1984."

"Hmmm...." Will pretended to think for a few seconds. "Michael Jackson?"

"Ah, Cadillac, what a sick sense of humor. Rest in peace."

"Since when are you such a prude? He died over one year ago, Skye, I think we are all over it already."

"I'm certainly not over it! And for your information, I'm an Irish Catholic now." Will scoffed. "See? You are ruining my birthday and I only have 3 more hours left to enjoy it."

"Jesus, Mary and Joseph." I heard him slapping his forehead, but there was a light streak to his voice I hadn't heard in a long time. "Where are you?"

"Sydney, knuckle head.   I'm off tomorrow on the cruise and I highly doubt I'll be reachable for a few months."

"Great! You always wanted to visit Sydney. What's the city like?"

"I wish I knew. I was so jetlagged when I arrived, that I woke up two hours ago thinking I was still in High School in Cleveland." Will laughed. "How's the baby? I don't hear her crying and it's what? 7am in Cleveland?"

"Yeah, she's at Sarah's." Separate bedrooms, look at Will, how modern. "Did you get my postcards?"

"Yeah, they are awesome. Thanks so much." It sounded like he was sipping coffee. "Sarah found a few a couple of weeks ago and flipped out."

"Oh shite, I'm so sorry." Why wasn't I really sorry? "Are you off to work soon?"

"Shit, yeah, did you say it was 7? I'm already running late, and I have a very important ecofriendly project to present today. I'm trying to raise awareness in the studio about sustainable architecture, but they are quite conservative."

"Wow, keep talking dirty to me Cadillac, I love it." I heard his soft chuckle halfway around the world, on a crappy hotel phone, and it was the best birthday present to me. "I'm proud of you. Are you nervous?"

"Are you kidding me? I haven't slept in a week. Whelan gave me a pill, propranolol I think, to take a little while before the presentation, but I'll try to deal with it medication free."

"You are going to knock their socks off, Cadillac. You are brilliant, and the kindest person I've met. And trust me, I've met almost the 6 billion people on Earth in these cruises."

"Thank you, Skye."

"Oh, and wear something dark, just in case you sweat too much." We both laughed. "And if that bunch of old good for nothings reject your ideas, I'll hunt them down and kick their asses myself."

He chuckled and sighed. "I have to tell you something, Skye."

Oh no, please don't let it be another baby. "Don't tell me you are having the second one."

"If by second one you mean mortgage, then maybe." I laughed in relief. "Nah, an almost one-year old girl is more than enough. This news I think you're going to like."

"Hey, don't be a jerk, I'm really happy you're a father. Your daughter is family to me, just because I haven't had a chance to bite her gorgeous chubby cheeks in person doesn't mean I don't love her," I said honestly. "But I think I know what you're going to say…" pause for dramatic effect, "…you got me the *Charmed Comics* for my birthday!"

"Got me," he said, as an alarm went off somewhere close by. I was certain he was lying, there wasn't something else going on, something major he hadn't had the courage to tell me over the phone. I would just have to suck up the curiosity. "That's my shower alarm. If I don't get in now, I'll get fired."

"Just marry me, you are too insane to be true."

He laughed again. "Bigamy…not exactly my thing."

"Why not?" I teased. "I can totally see you building an ecofriendly house for your harem of seven wives."

"Only if you are one of them," he answered, and another alarm beeped in the background.

"Go, go, I don't want to ruin your very important meeting. Good luck, Cadillac. Send me an e-mail as soon as it's over."

"Happy birthday Skye, I miss you more than you can dream." And I dreamt of him every night and every day, so *that* was a statement.

"I wish you were here," I said, hanging up the hotel's phone before I jumped on a plane just to look into his hazel eyes one more time.

CHAPTER TWENTY-ONE

ARGENTINA

December 2010

*A*ll I could see was the outline of her back, as she gazed longingly at the sunset, following our tradition. I had missed it for a number of years now, but I had always known she would never betray it. She would never betray *me*. She was sitting on a towel, the beach barely populated, with people scurrying off to get ready for their Christmas Eve dinner.

"We wish you a Merry Christmas, we wish you a Merry Christmas, we wish you a Merry Christmas, and a Happy New Year!" I sang horribly. Olivia turned around and goggled at me.

"For crying out loud, Lucy! My love, my baby!" She stood up and hugged me tightly, tears running down her face. "Oh my God, you crazy child, what the Hell are you doing here?"

"I thought I'd surprise you," I said shrugging. She held my face and studied every corner of every freckle. "We haven't seen each other in two years."

"And whose fault is that?!"

"Mooooom, don't start, please!"

She held up her hands in surrender. "Fine sweetie…I just missed you so much!" We hugged again and stayed that way until the sun was completely down.

"Mom, I need to say something, before we freeze to death in this desolated beach." I held both her ice cold, slender hands in mine. "I will never be the perfect child of your dreams. I will never be *normal*. I will always be like…this, you know. A little erratic, a little impulsive, a little moody, and a little crazy, I guess. I know I've come a long way, I know those 'littles' used to be much more than that. I'm still trying to figure out what the best version of myself is, and I've made your life incredibly difficult in the process…"

She stopped me there. "You are my reason for living, Lucy. I love you just the way you are, I never wanted you to change that, I just wanted you to be happy. I saw so much of your father in you, I was terrified…I wanted to save you from all that suffering."

"I think we both suffered unnecessarily."

"And whose fault is that?" she said again, raising an eyebrow, and I laughed. Mothers will be mothers. "Look darling, I've made my fair share of mistakes too. I was only 22 when I had you, barely 30 when your dad left. I was young and I thought that shielding you from the truth, from his past, from his family, would protect you. I'm sorry, I truly am."

"I know, I'm sorry too," I said, giving her a peck on the cheek.

"Your Irish psychiatrist once told me that what separated the two of us wasn't our differences, but our similarities. We are both so stubborn we can't find the right way to approach each other."

"Wordy woman, that one. But this talk might be the start of us speaking a common language." I smiled at my mom and gave her my hand. "Let's go, I'm starving, and you probably think I'm too thin for my own good."

"We have a reservation at 9.30pm in *Los Vascos*, as usual. The whole family will be there." She gathered her stuff and started walking towards our house in Mar del Plata, the house my mom, uncle and aunt had inherited from my Argentine grandparents, three blocks from the beach.

"Yazz! There's a huge plate of spaghetti calamari with my name on it."

*   *   *

"WHO.THE.HELL.IS.THAT?!" I whispered to my aunt Maria's ear. A tall, handsome man in his late forties entered the restaurant, and my mother instantly stood up and ran to his arms.

"Ben, your mom's boyfriend," Maria answered with a grin. "You missed a lot."

"WTF?" I mouthed back, but before she could respond, they were standing right beside me.

"Benjamin, this is my beautiful daughter, Lucy," mom introduced us in a strangely high-pitched voice. "Lucy, this is Dr. Benjamin Waisman, my boyfriend."

"Jewish and a doctor, I like you already," I said, shaking his hand. He grinned in response, and Maria nudged me a little too harshly, on my right side, thankfully.

"I'm a veterinarian, actually," he explained. He had a manly, enchanting voice. "I met your mother through her accounting firm."

She winked an eye at me. "I knew you'd like him."

"I think I love him already!" We all laughed. "Speaking of love, how was the wedding? I'm so sorry I couldn't make it, Maria, I was in Thailand."

Maria was sitting right next to her wife, holding her hand. They had met a decade back in a Psychology of Sports conference. Her wife, Rachel, being a Sports Journalist and Maria, a Personal Trainer, had both been there, and they had kept their relationship a secret until they decided it was time to openly embrace their love.

"Oh, it was really low key," Maria explained, looking lovingly up to Rachel. "No more than 50 guests, but we had a great time at the honeymoon in Cuba."

"I got the pics, they looked grand! Did you get my present?"

"What do you think?" said Rachel, both of them showing me the 18k white gold Claddagh rings I had sent them as a wedding gift, on their left hands, pointing to their hearts. I smiled broadly.

"Now, you tell us about your adventures," Maria prompted me, as the waiter served the entrées. Philip started digging into the squid rings with his fingers, and Greta, his mom, yelled at him to behave. Penny was busy texting with her new mobile, the twins were both 14 now, raging with hormones and unflattering acne.

"Oh well, we only have until midnight!" Maria's question called everybody's attention, and they were all listening intently to me now. "So, basically…I graduated as a chef," they all cheered, and Philip whistled.

"We saw the pictures on your Facebook…couldn't have hurt to invite us!" mom chastised me.

"And travel to Ireland for a crappy ceremony? Nah. I started working full time at a Dublin restaurant shortly after anyway, and then I went to work for an Irish Cruise Line Company in their kitchen for a year."

"Is that why you have that funny accent?" Philip asked, with his mouth full. Greta shot him a deadly look.

"Well spotted, young man." I gave him a high five. "I traveled through the Mediterranean first, then to the Baltic Sea, and I was finally offered a six-month contract around Southeast Asia. That's why I've been so…unavailable, especially the past year."

"How many continents do you know now?" Philip asked, his eyes huge with wonder.

"Five," I answered, counting with my fingers. "I might just take you with me one day." He grinned widely, and Greta scoffed.

"Sounds so amazing," said Maria. "I wish I had your courage, Lucy."

I squeezed her hand.   "And I wish I had yours. I'm really proud of you, aunt Maria."

"Are you still on the medication?" asked Greta abruptly. A dead silence flooded the table. So Philip couldn't be rude, but she could. Damn her double standards.

"Yes. Thank you for caring, Greta."

"And did you happen to find a boyfriend during these *crazy* adventures of yours?" she continued sourly, serving Penny a portion of salad. The teenager barely looked up. Benjamin cleared his throat uncomfortably and Bruno rolled his eyes at his wife.

"Nope, too busy focusing on my nutty self."

"Do you know who else is single?" mom interjected grandiosely. "Will!"

"Always so subtle," Maria mumbled through gritted teeth, and Rachel chuckled.

My heart stopped beating. "Wha, what?"

"Yeah, poor thing. They filed for divorce in August. His aunt told me," my mom went on to explain. Was she smiling? "That blond and him weren't meant to last, come on, it was obvious from the get go. Have you spoken to him lately?"

"For my birthday, the last time." I had suddenly lost my trail of thought. "Cruise…and stuff. I sent him postcards, but…you know… stuff."

"Right…maybe you should call," my mom suggested, faking elusiveness. And thank Father Christmas, the waiter came back with the main courses, leaving me alone to mull over my soup of racing thoughts, accompanied by a creamy calamari sauce, and a pinch of unexpected hope.

CHAPTER TWENTY-TWO

ALWAYS WILL

February 2011

" hank goodness that child looks nothing like you, Cadillac."

"Shit, Skye! You almost gave me a heart attack!" Will turned around and squeezed me in his arms. He was standing by a bench in Tremont Park, rocking a stroller with a gorgeous toddler inside. She had golden hair and big, turquoise eyes, very much like her mother's, Sarah, but without that fake, bitchy, Barbie aura. She had taken after Will's warm expression.

"Easy, easy, Schwarzenegger. I'm still a tiny, 12 meter-free fall Gold medalist...and you've gotten...bigger?" I pinched his biceps over his thick jacket.

He shrugged, giving me a hint of a smile. "Exercise is quite good for anxiety."

The snow had given us a brief respite. "I see."

"I don't remember if I told you, but I like your new accent, it goes with your curls," he joked, twirling a strand of my hair in his index finger.

"And I like your new muscles, they go with your..." The little girl shrieked happily and cut me off, but Will had gotten my meaning, since he had turned a deep shade of ruby red. "Are you going to introduce us?" I pointed at the oblivious baby.

"Right, yeah! Lucy, meet Violet, Violet, meet Lucy. You've both heard a lot about each other."

"Lovely to finally meet you, Violet," I greeted her in a stupid baby voice, grabbing her chubby hand. She screamed happily again and started pulling at my curls, shaking the tangled snowflakes to the ground.

"She likes your curls," Will said. "I like your curls. I missed your curls." A half Corgi-half Loch Ness monster puppy raced up to me, his tiny leash hanging loosely at his side. He jumped up and down my leg, until I had him in my arms. "Are *you* going to introduce *us*?"

"Shite! Aston! Did you do your business? We have talked about this; you wee naughty lad!" Will chuckled softly, and my heart plummeted to the snow. "Sorry, yeah, this is Aston Martin Charlie King the Second, Aston to friends and family." Will laughed and petted my dog's head. "He is three months old. We are still working on the toilet area."

"I can't say he doesn't look like you, Skye. I mean, the height, and all."

"Ha-ha! Arse." I punched him in the arm, and he pretended to be hurt. "I adopted him two weeks ago, you know, after…Philip. I just…needed some company." Tears began swelling in my eyes, and Will stepped closer to hold me in his arms.

"Why didn't you call me, Skye? I'm here for you, unconditionally," Will said in a comforting voice.

"I know, I really do," I wiped the tears with the back of my gloves, letting go of his arms. "But Greta didn't want to tell anyone about the funeral…" I choked up and couldn't go on.

"It's okay, I'm here, I'll always be here." Will caressed my cheek as I cried desperately.

"She was *ashamed*, of her own son! And Penny, she didn't even cry, probably not wanting to ruin her stupid make-up. I'm never talking to them again. I bet they blame me too."

"What are you talking about? They'd be silly to blame you, but you know, people react to pain in unexpected ways."

"People don't change their essence, Will, bad people will be bad, good people will stay good. That much I've learnt." I sat down on the bench beside us, playing distractedly with Violet's little hands. "That's what I'm scared of…I'm afraid this will be too much for me to handle, that I will spiral out of control again."

Will sat next to me and placed one arm around me, his warmth invaded my body. "You are not the girl you were when your father left, even when you found out he had died, Skye."

I reached into the paradise of his hazel eyes, mine all blurry from the sea of tears. "But what if I go crazy again, Will?"

"So what? You've faced and overcome your worst episodes of 'crazy' before, and look how far you've come." He cuddled me closer. "Every time something bad, or even something remotely new happens to me, I get nervous. I can't sleep, I sweat, I have palpitations. I worry constantly about the outcome. I obsess over every possibility. I feel insecure, not good enough. I'm an anxious person, I'm a worrier, but I've learnt to put a rein on it. It's just my brain, another organ, I repeat to myself. I have control over my mind, not the other way around. That thought comforts me."

I took a deep breath. "I wish I could distance myself from the pain and be able to reason…but I am so overwhelmed…I still can't make sense out of it, Will. Philip was so young, so full of life! Why would he do something like that? Why didn't he talk to me, to anyone? It's like I'm cursed with this insanity, and I rub it off on everyone around me."

"Don't be silly, Skye, you are so damn incredible! What Philip did had nothing to do with you."

"He hang himself with the bloody Playstation wires, Will! It's my fault, I taught him to give up, it was my example that drove him mad. He asked me to come back when I first left, five years ago, do you remember? And I didn't. I, piece of shit Lucy Skye, his big cousin, didn't. Then he saw me at the hospital in Galway, he must have thought I had jumped." I could barely contain my tears long enough to form a sentence. "I could have saved him, Will. Oh my god…"

"Lucy, look at me, look at me now." He placed his hand on my shoulders and searched my swollen eyes. "You can't think like that, torturing yourself helps no one. You are an example of strength, and resilience, and all the things one would want to be in life. Brave and passionate, smart and funny. That's how I see you, and I know for a fact that's how Philip saw you too. He looked up to you."

"He didn't deserve to suffer, my Phil…" I buried my face in my hands.

"Don't try to understand what he did, Lucy. You'll never find peace if you go down that road. Remember him for the lovely kid he was. He was lucky to have you growing up." He patted my hair softly. "I thought I wouldn't survive after my parents' accident, and then, so many other terrible things happened. Terrible things will keep happening to us, happy things will happen to us too, in spite of what we do or who we are. It's life. What matters is what we do with those experiences. If anyone can accept that, and learn to live with the pain, is you."

I blew my nose, nodding briefly. I appreciated his effort, but nothing, absolutely nothing in this world would bring me the slightest consolation, let alone, any sort of peace back. I would grieve for Philip forever. How could I ever mend my heart?

"Thank you, you've become quite good at pep talks."

He smiled proudly. "I read a lot."

"Divorced father of one and a hopeless nerd…perfect combination," I teased, still drying my tears. "Will you put up with me even if I go all whacky?"

"You drive me crazy in the best possible way, Skye," he said, staring at Violet, who was playing sweetly with a toy giraffe. "And for the record, I was a basket case before I met you."

"I seem to recall we met in a Day Hospital, true." We both laughed a little. "Divorced, a nerd and a nut job, I hit the jackpot!"

"Crazy is not such a bad word, Lucy. You always say it like it's an insult. Crazy can be brilliant, crazy can be different. That's rather good, in my book."

"And what a book you are," I joked. "Add wise to the list of adjectives, you might just be the perfect man. Marry me, once and for all."

He laughed heartily, shaking the giraffe to make Violet giggle. "You keep proposing so lightly, but be careful, one day I might just say yes."

I feigned disgust. "Ugh, what? And tolerate your tossing and turning every night in my new mattress? No, thanks!"

He chuckled. "Are you living with your mom? I doubt she'll be happy with him." Will pointed at Aston, who was rolling around the snow, Violet clapping in consonance. I couldn't help but smile.

"She's over the Moon that I'm back, but nah, I'm 26 Cadillac, and she's living with her boyfriend. Time to move on." I explained, holding Aston in my arms. "Besides, can you imagine Olivia cleaning puppy's gooey poo from her heels?" We both shook our heads. "So I rented a studio apartment downtown. I'm here to pick up some old stuff from mom's. And well, I happened to run into you."

"Destiny. Or have you been stalking me? That would be more like you."

"Don't flatter yourself." He smiled, stroking my blotchy cheek warmly again. "I start working in *Piazza*, that new restaurant, next week. I had the interview a few days ago, I got the call yesterday."

"That's wonderful news, congratulations!" Violet started fussing, and Aston was wriggling in my arms. Will dropped his voice and failed at sounding casual. "So I take it you are staying, this time around."

"If you give me a reason to." J.M. would kick me in the shins for being so impulsive. What the heck, he was worth it. Will withdrew his head from the stroller and looked into my eyes.

"Maybe if you cook for me. I hear you are pretty good," he answered, still staring at my face. My stomach wrenched with an unfamiliarly familiar feeling.

"Tonight then, Casanova. 8pm. My place."

He grinned, giving Violet her pacifier. "Just so you know…I hate fish."

"I remember, Cadillac, but I'm not making you a gourmet burger." He pouted stupidly. "We can settle on beef." Men!

"It's a date. Neither of us drinks now, so I'll bring a DVD."

"Please let it be Return of the Kind extended version, please let it be Return of the King extended version," I whispered loudly, with my eyes closed and my fingers crossed in the air.

"A little bird just told me it's Lord of the Rings: The Return of the King, Extended Version," Will answered, laughing. Violet began shrieking loudly. "I should take her to Sarah's, visiting hours are almost over anyway. Whatsapp me your address to my usual number."

"Whatsa what?"

"Oh geez, Lucy! Always in the clouds." He slapped his forehead and asked me for my mobile.

"The view is better from the sky." I looked for my phone in my handbag and handed it to him. "I'll send you a postcard."

He shook his head, chuckling. "There," he said, a few minutes later. "I downloaded Whatsapp to your phone, it's a texting service. Piece of cake. Welcome to 2011."

"Thank you, mister architect. We should get going."

"Wait, Skye." Will took my gloved hands and stared into my green eyes. "I need to say something." He took a deep breath and hesitated before opening his mouth, making my heart pound strangely fast. "I think I might love you," he finally spat, at an equal pace to my heartbeat's.

"Jaysus, Cadillac, took you long enough to figure it out!" I punched his chest and kissed him for what felt like the longest, happiest, most perfect second. "Don't worry, I think I might love you too." He pulled me closer and kissed me again, both giggling idiotically like a pair of insane teenagers. Insane, for sure, and proudly so. "Always have, and always will."

We walked away, hand in hand, my puppy to my left and his baby to his right, plunging in the sea of a new kind of healing and madness.

The End